The sun and the moon.

Both give light.

Copyright.

The sun and the moon. By Ngobeni Tlangelani ©2020 ChangePublication.

All rights reserved. No part of this publication may be reproduced, stored in a retrieval system, or transmitted in any form or by any means-electronic, mechanical, photocopy, recording or any other without prior written permission of Change Publication. *Any person who does any unauthorized act in relation to this publication may be liable for criminal prosecution and civil claims for damages.*

Cover designed by: Change Publication. Typeset in 14/11 Palatino by Change Publication. Printed and bound by Amazon LTT, services.

Tell:0735197861\0720700615. Email: Dauphumudzo@gmail.com

Contents

Acknowledgement…

I would like to thank God all mighty
for his amazing grace, for granting
me this gift. I will forever be
grateful for the love you have
given me. I give my gratitude to
all individuals who have
supported my gift, and push me to
pursue it. All your words of
encouragement and best wishes
has led me to write this book.

I dedicate this book to everyone who
will read it; You are one of a kind.

* Once upon a time*

THERE WAS A YOUNG GIRL; fifteenth of age, every day she would go and sit by the river that flows towards a young boy father's farm. Her name was *Hannah,* she was very fond to nature, she would take a pen, her journal, and went down by the river, at 16:00 P.M. She would put her legs inside the water, and watch as the sun goes down. By the time, she would be with her eyes on the paper as she wrote poems. Nature inspired her to write everything. She would express her feelings, sadness, happiness, and everything in between.

There was something about her; something no one could explain. Little did she know that where she sat every day, there was a farm boy who saw her every time she came. The young boy would just watch her, as she was watching all the beauty of nature. His life was in the farm, everything just resonates with him, and he loved there; he was just a farm boy. He would take care of the farm and ensure that it's all green. He took his Horse and wore the cowboy hat and went down to sit, where she would not see Him.

Time went by as they all did the same thing; it was the way of their living. One day, the farmer, slip and fell from the tree where he climbed and watch her. Hannah

just heard the sound of a boy
screaming, then she went closer to
look at what was happening. She
found a boy with his hand on his
leg which seemed very injured.
She helped him to stand up,
climbed the horse, and slowly
rode to the room where he lived.
She took a dish, pour some water,
and she went closer to him. She
cared for him, until he was better.
She never asked who he was
neither did he.

THE NEXT TIME she went and sit at
the shore, he came from behind
and watch as she wrote. The smile
on her face, and she was indeed
enjoying. He tapped her on the
shoulder. As she turned to look
around, she saw a face she had
seen before. He gave her a

handshake and said his name was John. However, she turned down her hand, and said she was Hannah, and then sat back to her spot. She continued to write, as if he was not there. He just stared at her, and he couldn't find any words to say after. She lifted up her face to look at him and they both locked eyes in shot… immediately both looked away, as if they were shy.

Days gone by, until the day where the weather change, it's nature and it rained. Hannah had nowhere to go, but in John's room. There they sat, and talked about their families, and what their hobbies were. As they were busy talking, getting comfortable with each other. The farm boy drew near to her and held her hands, put them on his chest, and whispered, *"an amazing young girl I've never met before, and I like you"*. Then Hannah sighed, she was having unusual feeling because she had never been close to a boy or a farmer in that way before. She let him go off his hands and ran straight to her house, she cared less of the rain. ***The farm boy*** stood by the door and called her, name, *"Hannah! Did I do something wrong, I'm sorry"*. She just looked back once and kept running.

THAT NIGHT she couldn't sleep, she kept on thinking about what happened during the day, she woke up in the middle of the night, and for the first time she wrote about love. But yes it's nature right? Then she was still in line, with her love for nature. She expressed her feelings through it, I suppose it might have been the longest or shortest poem she ever wrote. Cause no words could explain what happened to her, but something in her moved from that day. She told her mother about what happened, and her mom just smiled and said, *"baby that' is love, the boy loves you and you seem to have fallen for him too"*.

The boy asked his father to invite Hannah's family for a dinner so that he could at least see her. They did as they were asked, and both families met and enjoyed the dinner. Hannah and the farm boy walked out to went by the river, next to a tree where He felt, they laid down and watch the moon, and the stars, laughing as they tickled each other. They stayed there until the sun came out, still watch the sunrise together, and it was one of Hannah's dream; just to watch the moon or the sun with someone she could call a friend or a lover.

WHEN the summer came, the farm boy decided to ask Hannah to marry him, and she said, *"yes"*. They gathered together in the farm, and they tied the knot. The farm boy and a poetess rode on the horse, while she wrote poems for him every day. The time came that they gave birth to a little girl and named her, **Sarah**. They stayed in the farm and raised a little family, lived happily ever after.

Time went by, and Hannah was just a house wife. That's all she knew. She respected her husband and her traditions. Though people said that, '*sometimes people grow apart, it was never the same for the two*'. In the middle age, Hannah and the farm boy who happen to be named "*John*" would go down the river again. They sat at the same spot they first met. Hannah, wrote poems for John and little Sarah. Hannah took care of her family as a wife. John, was a father, and husband anyone could ever asked. Together they were happy.

When Sarah was growing, her father bought her a horse. He taught her how to ride.

She grew to enjoy life in the farm. Being daddy's little girl. She also had to learn extra way of living in the farm. She grew to understand that food came from the ground. When she was not in the house, she would be helping her father with the ground tilling. Together they made food from the farm. She helped her family. Not only she learned farming. Her mother taught her to express her feelings through poetry.

As time went by, her parents grew. Some of the things they could not be able to do, like they used. There came time, whereby she would do everything for them. Yet they kept their life doing simple things. The things they did when they were young, to rekindle their love. Like watching the landscape. An amazing thing of living in the country. Go see the poetry events. They also found the love of God, in a church nearby. Sarah, drove on the cart, to help her parents with visiting the medical practitioner, cause of their aging.

Due to aging, Hannah and John, would sit at the porch and watch the sunrise. Their legs trembles when they walk. They hold the sticks and on the other side hold each other's hands. They walk in the farm, watching the plantation of Sarah. Smelling the roses, and giving one to each other. They taught her well and they are proud of her. She became a young lady. And they wish she could find the love she deserves. It might not be the one they had, but love that will be forever.

Hannah fell sick, one evening. She was nursed at home. She decided that, she was going to remain in the farm no matter what. She said, "her peace was in the farm". And if there's a place she will die and be buried at, is nowhere else than the farm. When her sickness was deteriorating, John would hold her hand and pray. '*God you taught us about love and if this is her last days, I hope I will see her again, amen*' **will love her.** He would look her in the eyes, with love. Though he was seeing the pain in her eyes. He would still smile, and say, *I am happy I was loved by you, and I did too.*

On her last breath, she asked Sarah,
to hold a paper and pen. Though,
words could not clearly come out.
She was able to murmur the
words that made a poem for John.
He held her hand, she closed her
eyes. When the sun went down,
she was buried beneath the tree
that John climbed at his younger
days to watch her. John could not
have had a perfect life without
Hannah. Few days after her burial,
he was found peacefully dead in
his sleep. Close to him with a
poem that Hannah wrote. On the
other side, was a note, with a seed
to grow in the farm. He was
buried next to her soulmate grave
underneath the tree.

Sarah remained in the farm. Doing
what she was taught. All the days

of her life, she would still go by the river and write poems and she still took care of her father's farm and her family this time. Though Sarah would forget things. She would always find herself in poetry. But the greatest gift was that in poetry and in the farm, "love lived and will forever live".

All that I ever wanted

All that was before me, it's gone. My dreams are long lost. All that I ever wanted to be, just slip through my fingers. I had beautiful life in front of me. Beautiful and amazing. Everyone in town wishes their children were like me. I was a great example in my community. I brushed every boy away. Because I was building my life and making a good future. My parents were proud of me. I was on top of class. Teachers liked my determination. Every day I tried pursuing my dreams. Everyone could see the potential in me. *"Hey, Linda are you ok?"* Asks Malachi. *"Oh yes I am, okay, how are you?"* Linda replies, *"I am doing well, thanks"*. Malachi, I just came to say that, "breakfast is ready" *"Oh thanks, I'm coming downstairs now"*. Linda remains, standing next to the window. She watches as the bird's fly high. Imagining, how thing's could've been if she could just fly and never come back. Or maybe she's just watching her dreams flying with no courage to achieve them anymore. All is lost.

'She walks down the steps. She meets eyes with her mother. "Hey Baby, morning". Linda replies, *"hello mom are you good?"* "Yes, please. Cereal or bread", asks mom. *"Oh, anything is fine mom".* She sits in the kitchen chair. "Hey, anything! You sure?" *"Yes, whatever you are having today mom".* Mom, "I know you like cereal Linda". "What's going on my love? It's unlike you". *Well, "I'm trying new things".* She fakes that smile, that only lasts for seconds. Linda's mom, drying her hands, and putting the knife down. "I know you might have been gone for six months, but you will always be my daughter. I know you". *"Mom, Please! I promise you, it's nothing, all is well".* She looks at Hamilton, who sits in front of her. *"Haa, why are you looking at me like that?"*, Linda asks Hamilton.

"Oh me, no, no comment, young sister. Anyway, I'm going back to my room". "Mom, did you see how Linda is behaving?" "Eish son, she's like a new person". 'Whatever happened to her in college it really changed her'. Hamilton, with a serious face. "I know her mom, she is not doing well, something is off in her". 'Maybe it's just a mood-swing thing, she will be fine I guess'. Mom, takes off the apron she is wearing, "let me go talk to her". *"Please mom, Hamilton, holding her hand, let me be the one to go to her. I* know she will open up to me". *Hamilton was just three years older than Linda. So technically they grew up together. Picking on each other and playing pillow fight's every night*. "And you know that; I always get her back. No boy ever touches my little sister. I can fight tooth and nail. That's how much I love and know her. And besides we do share little secrets" He laughs as he climbs the steps to Linda's room. Mom just keeps her mouth open.

Linda is back under the blankets. And its kind' hot inside. She sounds like she's crying.

Hamilton, knocks at the door. "*Linda open, it's me your lovely brother*". Her voice inside; "shouting, go away I need to be alone!". Hamilton, "*please sis open, I want to talk to you, give me a chance*". "No, please, get the hell out of my

door!". Hamilton, *"sis you know,
whether you open this door or not I
am going to open it either way, Arg!"*.
Linda getting off her bed, she
unlocks the door. Hamilton sits on
the sofa, that faces outside, where
you can see people on the street.
He moved the sofa to face where
Linda is. "Oh, come on, don't do
that", Linda says. *"Oh, what do you
mean? You know I like seeing your
pretty, round shaped face"* he laughs.
She laughs also. *"Do you know how
beautiful you are when you laugh?
With those dimples"*. Linda, hides
her face with a pillow as if she's
shy. "Big brother please stop it".
Linda, "I'm dead serious"

So, tell me, what's eating you up?"
Hamilton asks. "Nothing honestly,
I'm just fine like this fish you see

here inside this jar". Pointing at a bottle of water with fish, in her head board. *"Sis I've known you since forever. Since we were young. Remember when we took dad's car and went off fishing, that's why you like fish. The tire got punched, and we get caught due to that. And When we came back you blamed it on me. He recon. Need I say more?"*, "Ok fine! No, stop I get it". *"Linda; mom and I we are just worried about you, and that everything has changed. What hurts is that it's not a good change, but you look weird. Like you are lost or lost something, and you can't live without. You hardly eat, you don't get out of your room. I mean when last did you get out the gate? Please let's go watch the waterfalls, your favorite place".* "I'm not in the mood", Linda says. Hamilton grabs Linda, "let's go". Put something, I'm going downstairs. You will find me there. We are walking not driving. Let's go see the bush. You need to clear your mind. And if I come back here, I'm just going to drag you and kick your butt off". He laughs.

Oh eish! Recite Linda as she put some Jean on and this huge jersey. Which looks like oversized. Hamilton has always been good to me. He knows me more than anyone in this house. He is my brother and friend at the same time. Maybe I can tell this secret to him. Maybe he will help me. I am overloaded. I feel guilty every day. My happiness is gone. Everything is taken away from me. I feel empty inside. I am full of shame, more if this comes out. I will be a laughing stock here in the community. Little miss perfect made a huge mistake. That's how I call it, yet I don't think it is. "Hey, Linda,

Anderson, come down here". Hamilton's voice from downstairs. "I am coming, she steps down and they walk out".

"Can you see, that leaf?", Asks Hamilton. "Yeah, what's the story Mr.?" With that attitude in her face. "You know one day; it will fall it won't be attached to the branches". "Yes, I know that", Linda responds. *"So it's like our lives, one day we are going to die, we going to*

lose the strength to hold on to what we've come to know as life. All I'm saying is that, we live once, and we can't live like tomorrow is promised. Live today and make the best of it, even when sometimes it's hard. Be grateful for the gift of life"." Ok Mr., I understand", she rolls her eyes as she looks around the bushes.

Hamilton, stands behind Linda, "*Sis, tell me the truth what happened or rather I say what is happening in your head? What's keeping you awake at night? We don't spend time like we used to. Just me, you and mom*". "Ok, fine, Linda, looks nervous. The truth that I'm hiding, is killing me, it's hard upon my shoulder. I can't do this anymore; I've tried my best". "Hey Linda", she shakes her head and finally come back to

Hamilton. She seems caught up in her imagination. Hamilton, *"please tell me dear"*. "Ok please don't judge me, I'm already judging myself and I'm overwhelmed by all this, so I need no lecturing, but a shoulder to lean on". Ok, Hamilton, sighs, and looks me straight in the eye

"I made a mistake; I walked the wrong path. I allowed myself to be deceived, manipulated and fell into all this temptation. Look at me I am nothing right now because of the choice I made". "Don't say that", Hamilton says. "Oh please, listen to me. I was naive, and followed the wrong voice in my mind. I got lost in the dark, I missed every good word of inspiration in head or I heard. I thought it would never happen to me. Today I lie awake swimming in my own tears. All that I went to college to take, I came back empty handed. But with something very innocent but yet came out of a non-innocent situation. What I did in the dark today comes to light, how Long Can I hide?", she deeply cried. Hamilton come closer to her, wrap his arms around her. She moves her head to find a spot, where she can lay head and feel safe.

"Linda, what's it? Don't cry honey", Hamilton, with his voice that sounds in pain. "Brother all I'm saying is that I am pregnant and the worst part is that the man is married. He has wife and children; how can I be so stupid?". She

again cries, this time, you can feel the pain she's been keeping inside for such a long period of time. Hamilton just brushes her back, and says nothing. "Brother, it's now over with me, can you believe? He even offered me money for me to do abortion. Now he even blocked my contacts. He is gone and I am stuck here alone with this little thing in my tummy". *"Linda, you are not alone, I'm here, as an uncle, and a brother as well so mom and Dad are here too. You know we will always be there for you"*.

Linda! mom's voice at the door. Mom "I know, Hamilton told me about your situation it's okay baby". She gets inside. "Baby we can get through this. And to be honest with you I am a little bit disappointed in you. But we have a future to look at. You are going to be a mother. You need to be strong for your kid. This kid needs you and your full attention". "But mom?" Linda, with tears falling like the waterfalls she loves to watch. "How do I tell him, why his father was absent, how he was conceived, that I made a mess, and this is the result? The consequence of my selfish decision". *"Baby we all have made dumb decisions. And what the kid must know is the truth only, nothing else".*

"How do I look at my kid? I will always have something to remind me of what I've done. How can I love the kid, when I will always hate the father? I was almost like a home wrecker. It's all bad. And this kid will be a picture I hate every day. Maybe I should have aborted this pregnancy like he said. Or its better I will put the kid to adoption". The reality, hurts her as her mind is filled with emotions that she can't shake off. "I'm done being hard on myself, I can't do this anymore, I can't stay here forever, I am going to get back on my feet and learn to live again. I am angry, I feel betrayed, used, lied to, taken for granted, and manipulated. He said he loved me and I believed every little white lie, he told me". She shouts! With rage; she tosses thing's on the floor. Hamilton come running and open the door quickly. He held her in his wide strong arms, and let her cry. *"Cry sis, take it all out, you deserve to be angry, to feel the pain"*. "All I ever did is to love him, but this is how he repay me". She sits on the floor, Hamilton sits with her, without letting her go.

"How are you feeling today? Take some protein. You have to take care of the baby", It's her mom as she gives her water to drink. "I feel better, thanks". "Your welcome baby, as she looks at her, I'm proud of you dear". "Mmh what do you mean proud? There's nothing to be proud of here, and you even said yesterday that I disappointed you". "Mom! Linda, yes I am disappointed in you, but I am proud that you are getting up on your feet, getting ready to be a mother. The past few days you've been doing well, showing maturity". *"Thanks mom"*.

"His name is, **Gift**, *because he is a gift from God mom*. I've never seen a beautiful thing like this before. I've never loved anything more than I love him. Look at him how cute he is. He is my blood. For nine months' mom. He's worth everything in life. Today as I hold him in my arms and breastfeed him, I know, I have a reason to live for. He needs me and I will be here every step of his way. I am his mother and I will be the father. I will make him proud". Tears falls on her as she talks, luckily it's tears of joy. Hamilton and mom just stands there, watches and listen as she speaks words of wisdom.

"Mom and Hamilton, I thank you for being there like you've always been. I love you guys. Hey boy, meet your uncle Hamilton and grandma." They come close to her and touch him as they welcome him.

Linda teaches him every step of life. From crawling around and walking. She teaches him how to speak. She keeps records of his life, through pictures and videos. At this point she takes time off the college to raise her **Gift**. Though grandma is there, she decided that it's her part to raise him, and that she will go back to school once he's bit old. Gift changed her life, and she never see him as a result of mistake anymore, but a wonderful creation. Once gift was able to go to school. She decides to go back to college to finish her degree in _Information technology_.

Everything has changed, her friends have graduated. She has to make new friends. But she chose not to, because she now knows better than before. However, there's one thing that has not changed at all. The married man who impregnated her and shut her down. He's still the same and there in the college. And the rumors about him are floating around. It's the way he is; she wasn't the first one. She walks in the corridor and crosses path, she smiles and walk away. He just stands, with no word in him, not sure what just happened. Maybe he thought she is broken. She focuses on her studies.

She even started a group of helping upcoming high school graduate, from men like him.

She *graduated* her degree with cum laude. She is indeed intelligent, despite what happened along the way. The community laughed but it didn't stop her from perusing her dreams of becoming an IT specialist. One day in her office, just after lunch. A man in suit comes in her office. The first thing he says is that, *"I'm sorry for what I've done and other young girls like you. I was selfish not to think like a good man. I disrespected you and played you. But it really didn't pay me well. I'm just an old man, whom my wife left, taking the kids with her. I lost myself in the process of my vanity. I am sorry. I want to ask to see your child"*. Linda, remain sitting, she stands and hug him. She then says, "I forgave you long time ago. Cause I would have missed the opportunity of raising your son, if I didn't".

TODAY, Linda is owning her own company. She is married to a pastor, blessed with other three children. And she never kept Gift from him. She just **Bows** her face every day and thank <u>God for all he has done and yet to do.</u> Sometimes when she visits her mom, she still stands at that window, and smile, all that I ever wanted is here. All tears stopped.

LOVE COMES AROUND

"Well, no Dad, I've been heartbroken by two men. I mean two. So, I'm done with those things". *"Lauren, you are just saying, you don't mean this".* "I swear by my mother's grave.

I don't need a man in my life they ruined me. Look at me, I am back at home to stay with my father. So ironic huh? So, Dad, if you are thinking of hooking me up with someone, please forget". Dad's laugh out loud. *"This stubbornness of yours. Simply shows me how much you need a man".* "It's not funny Dad. Just leave, you're getting late for work. Men are something else, they look you into the eyes and tell you that they love you. Only to wake up alone with a broken heart". *"Lauren believe me; you need love*". He slams the door laughing and left.

"I can't find my car keys have you seen them?" Lauren answers from the study room. "Check on the cupboard. You left them on the table yesterday when you get back". *"Oh yeah, I remember. Which side left or right?"* "Dad I know you just want me to come and give you straight". *"Well you are, my daughter so it wouldn't hurt to help me"*. He laughs.

"Oh, I'm busy, geez". "Are you going to keep shouting from there? Or you will come and show me". Lauren switches off the laptop, and drags her feet to give her father keys. "Here, take". *"You see, that was easy"*. He smiles at me, and I give him a long tired face.

"Hey that's not a way to be around your father. Today I'm going to be late, so lock the doors early". "I _am not 13 anymore dad_". "Really? What are you doing in my house? To me, you still are and always be". He brushes her shoulder; "I love you, goodbye". "*Bye Dad*", with unconvincing talk.

Now I just have to focus on my career, and writing my novels. It's all I can do. Relationships are not meant for me. I nearly died, when Timmy and Turner left me. But now I'm in a better shape. I don't think I will ever be in a relationship again. It's time consuming and worst part it hurt, when you give your all. They leave you with nothing. *Oh boy, who is calling now?* I push the chair where the phone is ringing, making a hell lot of noise. I just want to be alone. *"Hey girl? It's me trying to chin up, but I know I need my space now. Hey, Connie, how's your friend? I'm just calling to remind you about our plan today, 8 pm"*. "Oh, yah I even forgot. Ok I will be there", hanging up the phone.

I don't even know what to wear. A Jean or a dress. It's been long since I went out. But Connie is on my neck, I know she can't take no for an answer. I wish I can just call and cancel. But I know that she wants what's best for me. Just that I have so much to focus on. I have many cases to deal with. Being a lawyer, you have to juggle multiple tasks in order to make it in the court room. And here I have to finish this novel. And if I have to find a relationship, it will just not work. I can't be able to give him time. I just see a red dress; I can't remember the last time I wore it. Mm… still fit me very well, I'm going out like this. I have no one to impress. It's just a girl's out, nothing much. I took my father's other car Keys. I know my Dad won't be mad, when he finds me out. He has been pushing me so hard to at least meet somebody new.

Connie, she comes running to me. She jumps to hug me. It's been ages girl. Hey Connie. Connie is just a free spirit. I've known her since kindergarten. She always looks out for me. Even when I am wrong. *"So, Lauren, tell me, how are thing's going?"* Same old same old, how about you? She shakes off her head, so bad she can't answer me. *"Lauren I've known you for a long time. You can't fool me. I know that ever since you came back here, you have not been yourself. But you still look beautiful"*. She hit my butt and we walk inside the restaurant. I'm still doing my best in staying in shape. So, let me go for Greek salad with chicken breast halves. *"Oh, Lauren loosen up. Eat some junk and get some sleep"*. She laughs, Connie I have files of cases waiting for me at home so no. We then sit to talk about our childhood. So many memories. "Thank you

Connie, I missed this, you're a good friend". "_Arg don't say it, my girl, I love you_". She smiles, "I love you too girl".

Oh gosh, yesterday I slept like a baby. I step off the bed. As I check the watch, I can see that it's already late. I run to the kitchen. Only to find my Dad. "_Dad, what are you doing here?_" Well I suppose you forgot about me then. I'm making my own breakfast and for you. "_Dad you can't do this, no_". No sweat dear I'm still strong. Your mom taught me well. "_I know Dad_". I could see the change in his face. Though he always hides it with his big laughter. My mom's death still hurts him. He put my plate on the table. He put his head on the table. He holds his hands. I push the chair where he is sitting, just to be close to him. He fakes a smile and look at me; he wipes his face as if he was jogging, he says,

"**You** know, Lauren. My every day without your mom, is like a nightmare that takes my sleep away. I still miss her every day. I still wake up and look for her besides my bed. And sometimes hoping she will wake me up with a tray of breakfast. It's not easy my daughter. I say a lot of things, and get over thing's just like grasses as they fade away in time. _But no amount of time has been able to make me feel better,_ that she's gone.

And I even gave up in hoping that time heals. But with your mom I can't it's different. No amount of time has worked its magic". I just look at him, with tears in my eyes. "I miss her too Dad". We all do, baby. He hugs me so tight that I can feel safe again. He laughs, let me go before I get too emotional. But as he walks out, I could see that she lives in his heart.

Well, today I just feel like going out for an ice cream. I will deal with all these cases when I get back. I'm doing it old fashion way. I'm going to take a train to the mall, then come back as early as possible. As long as I get some fresh air. She takes the train and sit at the middle seat. I keep my eye on the phone, my mind is just so free and have peace inside. Finally, I'm over all the ups and downs. The train stops and I see this guy entering. He looks at me and we locked eyes. I quickly look aside, because many people get in and out. There's no need to assume the worst. It's a public transport.

Dad, walks in to the study room. *"Girl, how was your day, what did you do?"* Dad you're asking too many questions. But Fine I went to the mall, bought myself ice cream and got back home. So finally, you met someone. "Dad no, geez, I was alone". Alone, in the mall? You must be desperate my girl. I laugh out loud, like him this time. Anyway tomorrow I have a business meeting, and I want you to be there. Dad, you know I have lot of tasks, and besides I don't like business that's why I am a lawyer. Yes, you are right, I need legal advice in that meeting. He smiles and walk to his bedroom. Before you go Dad, what time is the time of a meeting? 8:30. Please, it's my sleeping time. Get yourself together girl, goodnight, love you. Arg, I hate this. I love you too though. I know, girl.

He closes the door.

I'm old now to drive. Says my Dad, but you can help me here. Ouch, I should not have come back here. It's too much. "Too much for your own father? What are you drinking?" He gets in passenger's side. So I can't argue anymore. I drive, and I switch on the music. We both sing along, and we just smile. *Though my mother is no more, my father has always been everything to me.* Our relationship never changed, after the death of my mother. Instead we have grown closer. And I love him so much. He's my best friend, we talk about almost everything. We got off the packing, switch off the car engine. We got in the meeting room.

After the meeting, someone comes behind me. He greets me. When I look at him. He's the same guy I saw in the train. Looking at me like crazy "coming Dad", I walk before he can even tell me his name. "Dad, there's this other guy". Mm a guy? That makes me happy. "No Dad that's not what I mean, please listen to me. I can't remember seeing him in the meeting, but I think he was there. I only saw him when we were done. He looks shy, kind, and humble.

With green eyes and little bit wide ears. He looks like he plays sports. A fine African man". Wow, a fine African man? Mmh. And what was he wearing? Dad asks, no I didn't really see it. But not very much suite. Anyway, it's nothing Dad, I told you I'm done. You can't be so sure baby. I pause for a while as he turns to walk out. Maybe he's right I don't know. It's been hours ever since I got out of the house. But today maybe I can go to church. My mom used to take me there when I was young. So I still remember few verses

Besides it wouldn't kill to look up to God. While I was still in my bed, I don't know what I felt, but the thing convinced me too much to go to church. I run to the bathroom. I put on a long, white dress, grab my bag. "I'm off to church Dad". What! you church? He sounds so shocked. You church Since when? Because its better ages? "Since I was little Dad".

Bye. I close the door with smile on my face.

I can still see the same door, building and all the trees that I left are still there, same way as it was when I left for Florida. It's been years since I stepped inside the church door. Even when I was in Florida, I never went to church. Maybe because of life in the city, it's very different from home. And it sure changed me. Not to mention those two men who broke me. But today feels good to be at church. *"Hey*

Lauren", I look to see who still remembers me here. Oh hi Mrs. Jackson, I come close to her. She gives me a warm hug. *If hugs gave meaning, I guess this one means, it's been long time.* Some wave at me. I can hardly remember them, though it's a small village. I suppose it has grown ever since I left. We sing all wonderful songs, luckily, I can still remember them. At least I don't feel like a prodigal son. Oh, I mean daughter. The only thing that fumbles me is to see the minister of the word. OMG, it's the same guy I saw while attending my Dad's meeting.

After three weeks, I have not been going to church ever since. I sit in front of the piano. I play as I sing along. I decide to play amazing grace. The song really makes me realize how amazing God is. I just see my tears falling on a piano. And I continue to play. I feel my spirit is revived. I start to pray, leaving the piano. I kneel down and humble myself before the Lord. I pray about it all out. The pain, hatred and anger that I've been keeping all this time. I feel so much relieved, and so loved. I just lay down in the floor as I let tears fall till, they can't come out. Though I can't recall the scripture, I know it says something about, *'come to me all those who are burdened and I will give you rest'.* And this is the rest I've been longing for. I feel at ease, my heart, my soul and my spirit, feeling connected to God…

As I draw nigh to the drawer. I open it, and take out the Bible. Its little bit dusty. I blow the dust away. I open it, I don't even know where to read. I smile. But the Lord knows. Before I can read anything, I open and finds a card with contact details. I even forgot who gave me, but I remember it was the pastor, the same guy in the meeting. I dialed his phone number and it went straight to voicemail. *"Hi, you've reached, Troy Bahman, I'm not available right now, please leave your number and name I'll call you back"*. Then tone beep, but I don't know what to say, or why I called. I am feeling a bit humiliation about all this.

Probably after a minute. I say '' hi its Lauren, Lauren, Michaels. I hang up. Something is fishy here. I don't know where I had this surname before, but isn't the first time. I left it and prepare dinner.

A telephone rings at 9 p.m., at least I'm still awake. I don't like late night calls. I pick up. **Its Troy**. We talk for almost 30 minutes. I pretend to be asleep, though he wants to go on talking. I hang up. It's surprising he asked me for a date. He doesn't waste time. But girl, I told him I will think about it, and give him a call when I am ready. He is such a gentleman, she says. "Take as much time as you can. I will be waiting for the call", he said. I continue to work on my court cases. There is this one case that baffles me, I even think of giving it or hand it over to one of

the colleagues or another attorney.
This is because I believe that this
case is too much and the man is
guilty. I hear footsteps in the
living room. Dad is that you? I
quickly rush to where the sound is
coming.

I stand, as I'm out of words. I see my
Dad's with his jacket wearing one
hand. His shirt is not tucked in.
He can't even stand still. He walks
from side to side. And whatever
he is saying God knows, because I
have no idea. "Dad, I though you
stopped drinking". Well he
replies, with his laughter, "I guess
you thought wrong". Because I am
drunk as hell. He is trying to
balance himself against beating
the walls. I help him to walk, and
sit him on the sofa. "Dad you can't

even sit properly. What have you done?" I really want to be angry but at this moment I can't. I have to be there for my father. I push him to walk to his room so he can sleep. I put him in the bed, take off his shoes, and cover him with the blankets. As I close the door of his room, I was watching him as he sleeps. I open and close the door and left. When I get in my room, I just pray to God that he keeps him. _And that one day he chooses to follow Go_d.

Though my dad has never been into church, he doesn't speak against it or stands as a non-believer.

"I am sorry about what happened yesterday", says my Dad as he walks towards me. Its ok, I say. Trying to keep peace between us.

"No Lauren it's not ok, I messed up big time. I can do better than that, I can". Do you want to talk about it? I ask my dad, who keep silent for a moment. Its ok if you are not ready Dad. "I can never be ready, but I think it's time. Sit down: 13 April 1992, I came back home. Just drunk like this or maybe even worse. I was angry from work; I was suspended at work. For something I did not do. Someone framed me. So, I went down to a bar. I drank myself too much. When I got home, I asked your mom to go out with me. She refused, because she could see that I was drunk. I forced her until she agreed. After 10 minutes in the road. I saw this huge truck in front of me. It was very foggy, I could not see well, and I was drunk remember. I thought the truck was coming straight to the same lane as I was. I drove off the road, I hit the bridge wall. The car jumped into the river. I only woke up in hospital. And when the doctor looked at me, she said she was sorry. I knew that my wife, your mother was gone. It was my fault Lauren".

I sit there, just look at my father. For the first time I see him crying. "I don't know what to say Dad". I am a sensitive person, but this time. I don't know how I am feeling. Maybe I should be crying. Do I console him. I honestly don't know. I'm feeling dizzy. I walk to the tap, and open it just to drink water without a glass. I calm down. Dad, I know you want me to say something right now. But this is too much to take in right now. "Take all the time you need, Lauren. But know that I am sorry, and I live with this guilt every day, it haunts me now and then. I took away my family and broke it apart. This is why, your brother *Henry* never came back after college. He knows what I've done. Now it's just me alone. Your mother was a good woman. She deserved better than what I did to her. Look at me, I try to live everyday like all is well, but deep down I am dying, cause that accident, I still see it in my dreams, though it has been over a decade".

"It's good to see you, thanks for calling me", Troy says, as his words is followed by a smile. It's a pleasure, I smile back. I was just feeling down, I wanted to get out of the house, get fresh air. "So, you didn't want to see me?" He asks. Well, you know, that's not, he quite me, "I understand its ok". After supper we leave the restaurant. We walk down the road, underneath the lights. "You are feeling cold?", He asks. Well, before I can even finish. He takes off his jacket and put it on my shoulder. This guy seems to know me more than I do know him. I say in my mind. As we keep walking, hey, you know there was this beautiful young girl. I went with her in kindergarten. One day the naughty boys, wanted to take her lunch box. However, I came through for her, and from that moment I knew I love her, and I still do. She sat in front of me in class. And during lunch I made sure no one touches her, and my name then. We graduated high school. I went for ministry. She chose college. "Whoa, what are you saying?", Your Brooks? Yes, they used to call me brooks. A quite one in class. Wow, and you still remember me.

Of course, *I never forget you*.

Dad, says Lauren as she walks to the kitchen. *"Can we talk?"* Anything dear. Dad I know you have been carrying this burden your own, and I know how hard that must be for you. I've been there, but for different reasons though. So, I forgive you for keeping this information for all these years.

And don't blame yourself. It's in the past let's move on. I will pray for you. "Thank you". We hug each other. So, what are we eating today? I ask my Dad. Lamb stew, cheese and macaroni. Well I'm ready. And I have good news for you. That day, the guy is, Troy. "You mean, Troy Michael?" The one and only Dad.

"Wow you got to keep him, he's a wonderful man. He owns a church, he is Pastor, and he is doing a great job". Duh I know, and we've known each other for a long time I just forgot him. But today he told me a touching story. He rescued me, when I was young…

Dad, I am going to a Wednesday service at church. "Its ok, pray for me daughter". I do always Dad. As I step out of the door, I see a car parked outside. When I give it a closer look. Its Troy. We drove to church it's been six months, since I and troy been going out and all is going well. Maybe he is the one. _I supposed love does come around._ "Do you see that tree?" Asks Troy, Lauren! oh hey, I'm sorry I was just thinking about something. I smile at him; because I didn't want him to ask what I am thinking about. "Its ok", says Troy, as he smiles back at me. Finally, we are here, let's get inside the church. At the end of the service Troy asks all members to remain in church, he has something to say. It's surprising he never say anything to me, but instead I remain calm. The pianist plays a cool song, and troy walks to me he kneels down.

''*Lauren Moyet, the first time I met you, we were both 5 years' old and ever since then I've been loving you everyday. When you moved away, I was scared to lose you. But I waited and here for you. Can you please make me the happiest man in the world, by being my wife*''?

I stand in awe, I closed my eyes and put hands on my face. I cry. Before I can say <u>yes</u> after tears of both joy and being scared. I see my father standing on a doorway. He nods. From that moment I shout, **Yes! Yes! I will marry you.** Troy put a ring in my finger. He stands and hug me so tight, and kissed me. I can hear the ululation, and clapping of hands. Troy then let go of me. I thank you all for making this secret, a success. Mr. Moyet, for giving me this beautiful flower. "So, everyone knew?" I ask Troy. "Babe everybody know that I love you". He smiles and lift me in his arms. How and when did you talk to my father? Well that's for you to find out, as long as I have you. He looks me in the eye, _"I love you, Lauren"_. I love you too Troy. We press our lips only to find that people are gone. Laughing.

I open the garage door and park a car. Dad, what are you planting now? Well girl, I just want to keep myself busy. I walk to him in the garden. He looks at me, with eyes that says, '' I am happy'' he smiles and stands straight facing me.

"Lauren I am tired, I am old. I don't have much time left in me". Dad, please don't say that. "Lauren its true, babe, you have to accept it. But what I want before I go; Lauren I want to walk you down the aisle. To give you to the Michaels family, to see you smile and be happy again. You deserve it babe. The second thing is to see your brother again, to I apologize to him. I hope he will come back before it's too late". It's okay Dad I will call him. No don't, He needs time. Maybe in your wedding he will be there.

"TODAY it's your big day", Says my dad, as he walks in my room. Dad you're not supposed to be here! I shout. Please Connie, you are my maid of honor, and you are letting him in. She laughs. Wherever you are I am supposed to be there as well. He forcibly opens the door, and laugh like all days. I am already ready like it's my wedding. Says my dad, as he kneels down. I turn a bedroom chair, to face him, giving my back to the mirror. "I love you Lauren, I wish your mom was here to experience this wonderful day". I know dad, I love you more. he takes a ring from his pocket, "this was your mother's ring. I think its best you have it. No one deserves it better than you". I hug my dad, we hug for a moment, I can feel him sobbing, please dad I don't want to ruin my make-up. He stands, I will see you at the chapel.

The music plays as I walk in the chapel with my father holding my hand. I see Troy standing there with the Bishop. He looks handsome more than ever. His eyes, when he looks at me. I still remember the day he saved me. It's all coming back to me. He has been loving since I met him. I wish I didn't have to go through all those heartbreaks. Maybe my life would have turned out fine with him. Family and kids by now. But I believe I have it now. I get where he is standing with the Bishop. I smile at my brother, as he smiles too. It's good to have him back here. My father let go of me and I stand towards to face the love of my life, Troy. We exchange our vows. The Bishop, announces Troy and I, Husband and wife. I could not have been happier than I am today, I tell Troy. Me too baby, we have bright future ahead of us.

Indeed, *love comes around, and God watches over us.* I continue to write my novel.

As next week, my book titled "God and Love" will be published. It's a story based on my life. All the cases I thought I can't deal with; well I did my best. Troy and I continue to minister at the Church. Life has been beautiful. My father lived with my brother till his last breath, he forgave him and he never went back again. Every time I look at Troy, his eyes tell me the story of when we first met. We are growing all together. Sometimes he helps me when my fingers can't play a piano. He knows I love it so much, but obviously him More. We've been blessed with three boys, and five grandchildren.

* I carry in my heart *
♡ ♡

"I am sorry I can't do this; you know I love you and I do know you love me too. But our situation is different. My culture, traditions as well as what I believe. It's not how you were raised too", Says Naomi, as she's even afraid of looking at him in the face. *"Baby look at me, and tell me you don't feel the same way"*, Randall, replies. Naomi, turns her face and look where Randall is standing. But she can't look him in the eye. She refrains from being close to him. She takes a one step backwards. He comes closer, to her but still she walks back again. "I am leaving and know I will always love you", as her voice cracks to say any other words. As she turns to walk, Randall grabs her hand, pulls her close. He put his hand on her waist. The other right hand moves on her face. Her eyes are weak. He says, *culture or no culture, I am going to spend the rest of my life with you, we can do this Naomi*. She nods, she leans on him, as that dark night flashes the moon. He let go of her. He blows kisses on the air. *"I love you"*, He walks away. She went back to the house.

Naomi! Dad's voice in the living room. I should go to him; she bows down before him. Yes, Sir. I and your mother have decided that it's good we leave this place. It's not good for both of us. More especially because of your relationship with that stupid boy. He is turning you into an immoral girl. "But Dad, I have not committed any sin, here". I thought you taught me to love. But now When I do, you are holding it against me. I love him, not the one you want me to be with. I know he has nothing; it doesn't matter to me. Be quiet! I am talking and you should listen. I've made up my mind. And you are going to do as we do it here. Are we clear? Asks dad, yes Sir. Go pack we are leaving tomorrow.

Mom, Naomi calls, "I'm here girl".
Mom can you please speak to Dad.
These arrangements I don't get
them. I want to stay here, and
have my life here. I want to have a
family here. Let me be please I will
go and live with uncle, **Steve**. And
besides I have to finish my ballet
classes. *"Naomi, it is already, done.
Your father has paid a ballet academy
where we are going"* You are going
to marry, **Rakesh**; he is handsome.
He comes from a rich family; you
will love him. "Mom please I don't
want to learn to love someone I
barely know. How are we going to
live together?" Baby it's our
customs, it's the way we do things
here.

"So, you mean because he is poor, I
can't be with him? Because he is

from the other side of the country. He lives at the Ranch. I thought love has no color or tradition, it's about a marriage between man and woman". *"Naomi! You are getting up on my nerves now"*, Mom's says with her face turning towards the fridge. *"I married your father,25 years ago. I didn't even know him then"*. 'Wow, you are going to pull that stunt on me, that was long time ago. Ok, fine, are you happy? Please leave Mom', says Naomi, with her hands on the table, bending over again. *"I thought so"*. She leaves.

"I wish I had a phone, at least I would call Randall so that I can talk to him. I know that even he stays far I can't go this late". Thoughts crosses her mind. I will

just write a letter and hand it
through a post mail box. I hope it
gets to him before we depart.

*Dear Randall, the first time you laid eyes on
me, I knew I loved you. I didn't have to
say it, it was written in my eyes never
saw any color, tribe or anything of the
kind I saw and still love in you. I am
writing this letter, with tears in my eyes
It's like a knife is stacked in my heart, I
want to let you know that I am going
back to Africa, my parents decided, I
wish I could stay. If we ever meet again,
I'll be loving' you, and by the time you
get here I'll be long gone*

Goodbye, xoxo, Naomi.

She put the letter in a post-mail box.
Hoping it will get to Randall
before she leaves the town.
"Naomi!", mom's voice from the
garage. *"Let's go it's time to leave"*.
She is leaning on the car. *"She looks*

at me, it's going to be okay, dear". How is it going to be okay? I am leaving the man of my dreams, my life is here, all for what? So, I can live your dreams not mine. *"Naomi! stop that, don't say things you will regret"*. No Ma, sounds furious, I am done, all my life I've lived for you, dad's expectations, what about what I want? Who I am.? You couldn't fulfil your dreams now; you want to ruin mine. "Get in the car!", shout dad as he enters into the garage. I flocked in and shut the door. The car hit the road…

"Randall, this is for you". Amy, says, handing the letter to Randall. "Who sent it?". He takes the letter in Amy's hand. "It's from, Naomi, why is she sending letter this morning?". He opens it. His facial expressions changes, as he reads it. His eyes couldn't take what is written. He folds the letter, and throw it as in giving it back to Amy. He runs to the stall. He saddles the horse. He put the trailer as he prepares, *Shonda* to go check on Naomi. "Hey, what's going on! Why are you acting all so awkward?" Amy, shouts. Please leave me alone, it's not a good time, I will explain later. He beat the behind of Shonda, so she can run as fast as she can. Maybe we can make it in time.

"Well done girl", Randall, brushing Shonda on her face. He got off from her. As he approaches the house, he can see that no one is there. The gate is locked. The dog is not barking anymore. He falls down on his knees. He cries so hard. He looks at the post box. Nothing in there. "_I lost her; I'm never going to see her again_". He speaks to himself. She was the one, my other half. My soulmate. But now she's taken away. His world stops from that day. He lost direction in his life.

Here, we are, settle down Naomi. This is your new home. You have to get used to it.

Naomi sits on the kitchen chair. Take, eat something. Mom's hand her an apple. She refuses. *"I hate it here, I hate everything. I don't like people making decisions for me"*. She walks to her room. "Girl, I understand what you are going through, but there's nothing I can do. Just listen to your dad's rules. And please tonight we have guests. Have a nice bath, and wear decently. Take that frown off your face".

Randall, please, you can't go on like, this. Man up! "Amy you have no idea what I am going through. She took a part of me when she left. And I know she loves me. And that letter she left, says it all. I knew the first time I met her that she is the one. When her lips met mine, I had no doubt that we are meant to be together. It's not her intentions to leave, but her parents". Leave the room. I want to read my books. Amy, I will find a way to fill my void in reading books. Reading the Bible. All I will do every day is keep on cleaning the stall, feeding the horses. This is my life now; my future is gone. But I will wait for her. I need her. But I refuse to accept that our love story is over. This is just the beginning; I will find her in my arms again. Another piece of my heart is with her wherever she is…

"Stay in your room, we will call you when the guest wants to see you", Says mom, as she closes the door room. She just stays in the room without saying any word to her. Just wishing she could turn into a fly. She would spread by wing's and head back to Tennessee.

At least it's a place I found love and happiness. After an hour or so. Mom's knocks on the door, "I hope you are ready?" She wears that smile of hers. Though I'm angry at the moment, her smile is beautiful and, when she does it, I just run to her arms. I walk to her and just hug and release some tears. She holds me, "tight, it's going to be okay, you will love him". We broke the hug and walk to the leaving room.

My father, sounds very happy. It's me, just by seeing people around the table, who seems to be having the best time ever. I'm here physically but my mind is somewhere else. I guess in the Ranch. Wondering what ***Randall'*** might be doing. I sit down on the mat. The guy whom my parents has organized for me, looks at me. A man I barely know, because we left Mumbai when I was very little. We lock eyes and I fake the smile, slowly fades and I start to cry. I got off and run, I can't do this, no. I locked my room and let no one in. I know wherever my dad is he is so pissed. But this is my life. The culture and traditions they are imposing on me. Aren't the ones growing up in. For heaven's sake, maybe if they didn't move us to Tennessee.

It's been, over 10 months', yet nothing has changed in me. I still feel the touch of <u>Randall</u> in my body. Those sweet lips when he kisses me. I still hear his voice when he says *I love you*. Those Blue eyes when he looks into my eyes. Sometimes I still melt, when thinking about him. I know I love him. But now it is just a memory, a dream maybe. I'm so lost in this place. Sometimes I just look at the window, and wonder if someone can see the pain I'm going through.

Hi, I'm **Rakesh**. Sure, I'm Naomi. It's after the third dinner they prepared at home. Now they say I should get to know him. Arh! such a drag. He talks like no body's business. He talks all the time I am with him. I just nod and fake smile. I wonder how he even feel about all this. But I guess he is fine. Cause he is here being so positive about our marriage and having a family. We just do the same thing every day and it's not like me. He brings me flowers and buy me gifts, yet he will never be like **Randall**; Randall didn't have to try to be anything. He was just himself and I loved him the best way I know how.

"Do you like him?", Mom asks as she comes close to the steps where I am sitting. He's fine. I reply. *"You will love him with time"*. Mom can I ask you a question? Anything my girl. "Do you love dad?", Naomi, this is not about me, I mean you've been together for a long time, yet you can't say you love him. Here you are telling me that I will love him. At least for Randall I had no doubts. *"Stop talking about Randall, he is not here"*. You are not going to see him again. If he loved, you the way you say. He would have searched for you, and be here. But now, there's a man, who wants to marry you.

"Mom, isn't all about marriage, not all of us believe in this thing's, maybe I don't want to be married". "*Stop it*", she slaps me on my face. I sit with my hand on the face, and she walks down.

I think of what my mother said to me earlier on. Maybe it's true Randall doesn't love me. I mean now it's been a <u>year</u>. And no word from him. I'm stuck here with him on my mind. He promised that wherever I will go, he will look for me and find me. Maybe he is searching or even given up. Maybe I'm better with, **Rakesh**. He is here, trying the best he can. Though I always give him a cold shoulder; he is patient with me. I guess Mom is right, I will learn to love him and together we will build a family. Tears falls, as I'm caught up with not knowing what to do. Which mind to listen to. But this is not my intention, it's tradition I'm forced to follow. What choice do I have? I'm just going to listen to my parents. Ceremony is in two days so I have to marry that guy against my will. But Randall will always be my first love and nothing will change that.

Finally, we got married. The uncomfortable part is that I have to share a room with him. I am his wife now. I have to perform wife's duty. Including, making love to him. I mean of course I will fall pregnant. What if Randall comes back? How will I explain. Maybe he will understand. I choose to

sleep with a pillow wall. To avoid
anything at night. We continue
like that for several months. My
parents are always on my neck
about grandchildren. I mean even
making love to him, I don't want
to. Cause I will be thinking of
Randall. He knows me better than
anyone else. And I promised to
make love only to him. So, this is
all burdening to me. Fortunately,
he has never forced me to make
love. He keeps saying he will wait
until I am ready. He is a good guy.

"Naomi", says Rakesh with a soft
voice. I know you don't love me,
but we are married and I am
trying here to be the man you
deserve. I am not Randall and I
will never be like him. But at least

give me a chance to love you the way you are supposed to be loved. I am loving you, and I will be a better father to our kids. We will have a family.

Please think about it, I understand you, but what I don't is why you keep pushing me away. It's been seven months. I haven't touched you, not even a kiss. He sighs and stand up to leave. As he is about to close the door, *"Rakesh!"*, I follow him to a door. I spread my arms, and he let me in his. *"I will try, I'm sorry"*.

Rakesh, looks at me differently. He might not be Randall but at least his love is also pure. Not many men can be so much patient with all that I've been doing to him. I leave the kitchen to where Rakesh is sitting. He is watching the news. I don't even know what to say, but I am willing to try, he deserves better. *"Hey, do you mind if we take a walk"*. He smiles and says no. I took off the apron and wash my hands so that he can tell me the history of Mumbai, and all that excites him. At least this time I'm also sharing my Tennessee upbringing. When we get home, we sit and watch TV having our first kind dinner together.

Slowly I start to not over think of Randall, but he will always be in my heart. Rakesh is a gentleman. I like him a lot. We are living like a married couple and I do enjoy his company. He does lot of staff at home and he play his role very well. Time went by, and we even start kissing, one thing leads to another. _Until we both understand that we are indeed married_. I do think about Randall, but Rakesh is that man that every woman wishes to find. I feel safe with him. Sometimes when he's holding me, I feel like it's Randall, and I can't let him know that. But I suppose he can see it through my face. He knows me, he knows how to lift my spirits up.

"Hey, Naomi 'would you like to go with me at the cinema? There's this new movie that I must see". He speaks from the bathroom. I laugh, man finish your bath first. 'Oh, you can join me if you want, I will show you my dance moves'. He laughs. After we are done. He drives off to the cinema. As the movie is in action, I keep leaning on him, on some scary parts. This was amazing, I look at him, *"I thank you Rakesh and I love you"*. Wow, did you just said you love me? He moves back and holds his nose and mouth. "Yes", I nods I mean it.

I am sorry about everything that I put you through. He looks at me and laugh so hard when we get home, because I was even afraid of getting out of the cinema.

IN THE MORNING, Rakesh, asks me a question. "Did you saw that African guy who kept looking at you?" No, I didn't. Even when we were leaving, he was behind us, as if he wanted to talk to you. Maybe he thinks you are someone he knows. Says Rakesh. Maybe, I mean I have been in Tennessee, African men are many, and I don't think one of them moved here. Well, let me go prepare breakfast. "What do you want today?", Naomi asks. Oh, anything honey. I'm hungry from last night laugh. As I prepare breakfast, something clicks on my mind. Maybe the African man is Randall? I immediately shake off the thought, he can't be here no.

Baby there's someone at the door. Says Rakesh. I know once you sit in front of that TV, you're like a glue, you can't get up.

"Yes, you know me well sweetheart", he laughs. I open the door. I couldn't believe what my eyes is looking at. Rakesh, from the sitting room, who's their baby?

No, it's fine I close the door. I didn't want Randall to come where I am. *"So, your married?"*, Randall asks as he plays with hands like he always does, when he is not feeling good about something. What are you doing here? I ask, feeling all this nervous. I shiver as like an earthquake moving the grounds. He looks at me and say, *"I am just passing by"*. He takes the contact card and give it to me. I slowly accept it. As he is about to leave. Rakesh comes to the door. He greets Randall. "Oh hey, the man who could not keep his eyes off my wife", He boast. Randall smiles and says, "nice to meet your sir".

My love, ever since that guy showed up in our house, you are no longer the same, who is he? Well no, babe, don't be silly. You know I've just been busy. I mean, I have lot of things in my mind. Ok, says Rakesh. I know him, once he says okay. He will never talk about it again. But I think he deserves the truth. At least I owe him that much. He has always been there for me and he knows that I was in love with someone else whom I never break up with. But the circumstances, forced us to part ways. Dear, says Naomi. Come sit here I have something to say to you. Ok shoot, he laughs like he always does. He's a happy soul. And he taught me to be happy too. I love him dearly…

I pick up a phone, to call Randall. I have to see him. I went down to a restaurant, where we are supposed to meet. As soon as I enter, I see him at the corner. He is wearing his old boots; the ones his father gave him. His brown cowboy hat, hides his eyes. I sit next to him. He lifts the hat so he can see me. Hi cowboy, says me trying to make him feel comfortable around me. The guilty conscience hits me hard. When I think of all the promises, we made to each other. He calms down like he always does. He looks at me, with those blue loving eyes, the way he used to. Everything in me moves, and I just want to embrace and kiss him now. But I am a married woman.

Naomi, I made a promise to you, you know I keep my words. When you left me everything stopped. I lost myself and I have never found anyone like you and never will I.

You're the one I've always loved. Randall, it's been five years, I didn't know what to do. And many things have changed. I respected my parent's traditions. Randall, it's okay I understand. *"If it's him you love and makes you happy. Be with him. You deserve to be happy. I will be waiting for you"*, Goodbye. Tomorrow I'm going back to Tennessee, I just wanted to see you and I have. Take care. He kisses me and leave.

Me and Randall come a long way and when I saw him today. The love we have, just started over again.

Rakesh, *"so you are still in love with him?"* I can see it in your eyes.

When you mention his name, you just can't hide it. I know we have lot of plans. A good future ahead of us. And you've been happy around here. But I can't let you stay here against your will. We've been together for five years and though you learned to love me. You love him more. You do have true love; I know what you told me about Randall. I mean his home town and poverty, yet you loved him. I respect that.

Here, I am stuck, I don't know what to do. I mean I love them both. But I can't be with them both. What frustrates me is that they both want what's best for me. They are willing to let me go. I guess it's what they say. *"**When you love someone, you should let them go**"*. Rakesh hasn't said a thing ever since our last talk. I guess it's his way of dealing with everything. I also haven't call Randall. But here Rakesh, can see that I am no longer here. Here with Rakesh everything is going so well. But when I think of college with Randall, our future, kids in the Ranch it's just all so perfect too.

"The tension in the house is just so not good for us, Naomi. Don't do this to us". Rakesh calls me in the kitchen. He sits at the table. I stand in between his legs. He holds my waist and bring me closer. He stops as I hit the table. He looks at me. *"Naomi, thank you for loving me.*

You have my blessings. I will always love you. He starts to lose his words. He can't say other words anymore. He just leans on my breast and I let him cry. I cry too. This is hard for me Rakesh. Don't say a word I understand. Just say you love me. I love you Rakesh. He stops her. It's enough. It's all I wanted to be here. I bought you a ticket to Tennessee, you are going to leave in an hour. I packed your bags.

* Raising my little family *

Paul got a job and this is a dream come true. He screamed out loud. As an expression of Joy. And hung up the phone while hugging Mercy. Little Johnny was just roaming around the house. Paul lifted Mercy as his huge arms covers her. He taps her hair to the back, and kisses her, so soft and warmly. He tells her that he got job of his dream. To be a soldier and fights for his country. Mercy rejoices with him, but her heart races. Thinking of the risks in going to war. The chances of getting back are very slim.

Other's go and never comes back. Or at least injured. You never know, what actually happens to them. But Just lie awake, hoping one day they will show up in the door step. This thought runs in her mind before she can say anything to him.

Mercy calls, Paul. Did you hear what I said? *"Mercy oh yes, sorry, I'm just not sure how to respond to this".* Babe, you know it's my dream, I love it. Mercy nods, *"yes you are right I know, and I support your dreams, Hun".* Please can we talk about this later, I must take Johnny for a walk. She steps out of the door. Her hand on head, touching her hair.

She seems very lost. The news didn't really please her. She went down the road, and just crossing, at Both directions. She wonders until she gets tired. She even forgets that she says she is taking Jonny out.

AFTER about an hour she comes back. Hoping she is calm by then. She walks in the office, where Paul sits. She knocks and draw closer to him. Her voice trembles. Mercy says, *"Paul? What does this mean for us?"* Paul, replies and stands from where he is sitting, "Baby what do you mean?" I mean this; what we have here. Look at me, I am pregnant and Johnny is just a little boy. Are you going to leave all that behind? *"Mercy please, don't start, why can't you just be happy for me"*. Hell yeah of course I am, and you know that, but what am I suppose to do now? How do I raise all these without you? You know in few weeks I'm having twins, she sighed, and breathe like she needs some fresh air outside. Paul walks to her, hold her hands, *"please come down. We can do this babe, it's only for few months. I'll be back before you know it, I promise".* She sits on the chair, where Paul sits. Ok! Okay, but I am not happy with this.

Paul, opens the curtains as the sun reaching out the horizon. ***Morning sunshine.*** Paul's voice waking Mercy. She pulls a blanket off her face. Paul brings breakfast, she sits on the bed, she yawns. Before she can dig in. She takes sweet apple juice in a cup. She holds it as she takes it to her mouth. But before it can reach her mouth, she asks. "So, when do you leave?" Paul holds his breath. He sits next to her. Taking the tray off the bed. Mercy asks again, I asked you a question, is it hard to answer?

"Mercy please, stay calm dear". Just tell me when you really going, she yells. *"Tomorrow afternoon, okay"*. Mercy, breath in and out. She asks Paul to leave the room. She says she needs time alone. Paul listens and straight vacates the place.

Baby, you are not eating, you barely get out of the bed. It's not good for the twins. "What do you expect?", Asks Mercy? My entire life is here; our home is here. And now you are just leaving me out of nowhere. She holds back tears. But she fails as she thinks of how life was, back then. Being raised by a single mother. She put her hand on her waist, with one on the head. Moving forward and backwardly *"Baby, I know raising kids alone is not an easy thing. I* *know, my mother did it. While my father walked out like you are doing".* Whoa, Mercy, I am not anything like your father. I love you and the kids. I will never abandon you, or the kids. You are my life. And this, I'm doing it for you all. It's for the good cause. When I come back, we will move to our new house, downtown and send the kid's to private school. We will then spend time together forever. "How long do we have?" Asks Mercy? 14 hours it's all we have now. Let me check on Jonny then I'll be here with you till, sunrises.

"Hi, Baby", Paul in the **MORNING**. "Hello" replies Mercy. But you can still hear sadness in her voice and grief as in her blue eyes. Paul in his deep voice, says, "Mercy I am sorry it comes down to this situation. And I want you to know that, I will always love you and the kids, you are my priority. I meant every word when I married you. I am not forsaking it now. Wherever I go, I have you in my heart". He opens the drawer and take a picture of her and him together. He cuts it until you can only see their heads. He opens a necklace with a shape of love. In that necklace you can open it in two pieces. He places the photograph inside that necklace of love and close it. He puts it around his neck. He looks Mercy in the eye and say, *"no words can explain how I'm feeling about all this but I'm feeling love for you and never doubt that"*

Mercy holds little Johnny, on her arms. Paul kisses them both. As the car wait for him in the drive. She sniffles and closes the door and sit down behind it. She asks Jonny to go play in the living room. She cries herself so hard, and she didn't want to do it in front of the kid. She gets herself together, she can't lose the twins, they are peace of Paul. She looks at Jonny and smile. She hugs him, and tell him, you remind me of your father and I love you so much. She knows that no one can replace him, he's just a kid, he doesn't understand my pain. But he can sense, cause everyday he asks about his daddy. He wants him to read him bed time stories again. Someone with big voice to tell him everything is alright. He still has some nightmares and Paul isn't here.

OH, slow breath. Mercy pick up the phone and calls 911. When her time finally comes, she brought forth the twins, a Boy and a Girl. They are so cute; she smiles as she's holding them in both her arms. Fortunately, they have agreed on the names. *Amelia and Don.* She finds comforts in them. Yet the truth still kicks in, when they cry in the night without Paul to help her. Now he's gone, no one to help me. She still cries herself to sleep. She still thinks he chose his dreams over family, and at night she keeps looking, hoping, he will open the door. she wishes to see his car in the drive way. The lights

keep turning on and off in the
neighborhood. But no sign of Paul.

Paul promise to call now and then.
And at least write a letter. He did
that only for few days. He can
easily forget about his family.
However, Mercy keeps on writing
and sends letters to him. Letting
him know the growth of the kids,
And their well-being. But she
never receives anything from him.
This kills her every day. When
Paul left, it broke her heart. She
never gives up on writing, hoping
one day he will respond. Days
gone by and nothing, call or letter.
And as she watches the news, she
hears about all the tragedies that
happens to soldiers out there. Her
heart keeps pounding as he
crosses her mind. It's bad not

knowing where my husband is, what's happening with him, or maybe he's already dead. She bang's her Hands on the kitchen table, with anger inside.

It's been five months, since Paul left. Nothing much has changed but raising the twins, keeping her mind off Paul. Yet looking at Jonny her heart just breaks into two. Every day he is asking why he did this; the twins don't even know him. Maybe for them it's better, because they were never around. But for Jonny it's hard, as he is learning to do things without him. The thing's they did together. He's missing every step of the twins. He still thinks about him every day and cries at some point, wishing he could be here.

Two days' way, Daddy is supposed to be here kids. She smiles as she speaks, her jaws filled with joy. But it is hard to be so sure cause he hasn't called or say anything in a while. These thoughts running in her head, wipes the smile off. The rain in her eyes that keeps the sun away. The thunderstorms inside her heart, if something happens to him. She prepares the house, so when he come back, he will feel at home indeed. The phone rings on the other side of the house. Mercy runs to answer. She hears, "Baby I'm coming home", on the backside of the phone. *"Paul is that you, Hun?"* She couldn't believe what she was

hearing, though she knows, that
his time is done.

She thought otherwise. She's only a
human, it's fair to think this way.
"Yes, baby it's me'", Paul answers.
She hangs the phone and thanks
the Lord, with a loud voice. She
runs back to the kids and hug and
kisses them. She holds them so
tight; she celebrates. Just one
phone call, that she's been waiting
for.

She counts hours and he call to say in
an hour I'll be in town. She sits on
the porch with the kids, waiting
for him. She looks at the twins and
says, "*today you will see daddy for
the first time*". She smiles and
brushes their heads with her hand.
She kisses them on the cheek.
Jonny means everything to her,

though she loves twins as well. Jonny was there when Paul left, and it was him that reminds her of Paul. He's Young but somehow understand my dark days. He comes and sits next to me and says nothing. It's who he is, not talkative but very supportive and courageous.

The hour passes and no sign of Paul. Unfortunately, she can't even call. He used private phone to call. The sun starts to get dawn behind the mountains. The cold approaches. She takes back the kids inside the house. Jonny starts to ask, *"where is Daddy?* You say he should be here soon". She draws him in her arms. I wish I have answer Jonny, but I don't. Let's wait for him. Frown weighs her face, as she tries to be strong for the kids. She opens BBC News on the TV. She still doesn't know why but somehow, she switched it on. She keeps her eyes on the TV like a glue, with no brows moving.

Something inside her just didn't feel right about Paul not being home already.

She covered her body with her own hands. Trying to maybe hug herself. She is shivering. Tears keep rolling. She already given up in wiping them. The kids are just crying at the other room. As for little Jonny, he sits close to mommy. She takes him in her arms and she cry so hard. She can't stop thinking about what she saw in the news. When a plane that crashed with many people dying immediately in the scene. People who were flying back from, Afghanistan to meet their loved ones. Mercy never think otherwise; she just concludes that Paul is one of them. The phone keeps ringing, yet she can't pick it up.

"I miss him, I miss the father of my kids, I miss my husband". Mercy, talking to herself, as she stands next to the window, holding a curtain. Which helps her wipe her tears.

IT'S BEEN SIX MONTHS since he died in a plane crush. It's been a year since he left us here alone. Me and the kids. I'm enraged, this is not the life I had in mind. Yet the pain never changes, nothing is moving. Everything is falling apart. How do I explain to the twins? I wonder if Jonny can barely remember him. This dream of him brought so much grief and sorrow. She kept thinking and just cry. It's never easy. He should have taken another job not this one. We were happy, we were fine, we were fed and had a roof. I have given him kids, family, home, he had somewhere to call home. I was there.

THE NEXT DAY, she sits in the sofa She watches the kids playing. Where she sits and talks and laugh with Paul. All the memories just reminded her of how life can be cruel sometimes. She hears the sound at the door. She moves elbow to dry her eyes. She walks towards the door. She opens it. She sees, two men standing in her door. *"We are sorry for your loss mam, our condolences to you and your family"*, one of the gentlemen says. She nods, and says, "thanks". This is what we found; we believe it belongs to your husband. She receives it. It's necklace he wore the day he left. With that lovely picture inside. She holds back tear as she opens it. "Are you okay mam", officer asks? Oh yes, I'm sorry, thank you.

IT'S BEEN FIVE YEARS since he's gone. But time isn't making changes in this pain. The kids have all grown and very much responsible. But though he left, his presence is forever missed. It's hard to have someone you love, being dead without knowing

where they have rested. No grave
to go to. Only the pictures, but
inside my heart he lives. Though
his money is here and managed to
buy a new house. Move to the city.

Take the kids to private school. It's
what he would've wanted. She
remembers, it's what he said when
he was leaving. *"Oh Lord I certainly
did that"*. But pain, shutters here,
and she tears roll down her face.
The one thing again he wanted; to
be with me forever like he said.
That I can never fulfil. She cries
harder, the thought of
unachievable dream.

Mercy remains true to her vows. She
resides in her home. Johnny is all
grown. He is reminding her of his
father every day. Instead of going
to a far college. He chooses to

study next to home. Where he will
help his mother, raise the twins.
She is trying her best to smile
again, but at times, memories of
Paul get toll of her. Maybe it's
because love never dies. She forgave
him, and looks on the kids and be
grateful, though he's gone. He left
a living memory behind.

Mercy never gets courage to remarry
again. But her family grows
bigger. Jonny got married and
have kids of their own. Though he
wanted to move back to the
country, his love for his mom,
urges him to stay. Don also is a big
boy and very naughty. He
impregnates a girl. *Amelia,* she's
just so beautiful and a very
wonderful young lady with good
manners. She takes after her

mother, she laughs. With three grandchildren she's is a happy grandma. Though Paul died without seeing his family again. Mercy knows he died a hero to the world. She wears the necklace till today. When she thinks of him, she just presses it on her heart and whispers. I love you and smile.

* Mandy and Ai *

IT'S SUMMER AFTERNOON, when Mandy is walking in the garden. She sees All kinds of flowers. They all look beautiful and sweet smell. She is here to pick up a white rose. She does that every once in a month. She ensures that she get a fresh cut from the garden. She takes it to her mother's grave. It's a memory she never forgets. She prefers a white one, because it was her mom's favorite. Her mother would cut it and give it to her, as an expression of Her love to her. Her mother died When she was very young, due to some sickness. So, she walks looking for a wonderful rose. The one that suits her mom, this month. It must be the most beautiful above them all. Not only because she misses her, but because it would be her birthday today.

She is happy listening to her mom's most song they played together. *'I hope you dance'*, by Lee Ann Womack. She tries to keep everything that her mother used to enjoy in her heart. Her memory lives within her. Though, this day may be one of the most painful day. She somehow has accepted the reality. She moves inside the garden, with headset in her ears. Before she can be close to a rose which seems more blossom. She hears a sound, just a meter from where she is standing. She took the headset off so that she can hear more loudly. The sound keeps lowering, the more she listens. When she draws near, she sees a little puppy. He is stuck in a mud. It rained yesterday. He might have lost his way home. Maybe the mist humidifier filter blinded his way. She kneels down and, lift him up. So gentle, because he is even wet and seems cold. It can only mean he was there almost the whole night.

She takes him to the house. She
cleans and brushes him. She
places him in a safe and warm
place. She runs again to the
garden. She has to be in her
mother's grave. But she had to
save the puppy too. She cut the
rose. She locks the house and gate.
The sepulcher cemetery is not very
far from her home. She never
bothered to drive. She gets in the
graveyard. She bows down. She
kisses the white rose and nicely
place it in her heart before she
puts it in the grave. A tear drops.
"Mama I miss you every day. I
know one day we will meet again.
I love you. I hope we will dance
again together. I know you are
watching over me from heaven. I
have good news; I might have
found myself a new friend. We

will talk about him when I come again". She rushes off to home.

When she opens the door, little puppy still where she left him. *"Hey boy, what is your name?"* Asks Mandy, she smiles. You must be hungry; it's been long since you ate, I guess. She walks to the kitchen, looking for something she can offer a puppy. She doesn't even know what she can prepare. It's her first time being with a puppy. Thanks to the internet. She quickly browses through Google; she searches for kind food for puppies. She has to go to town to buy food for a puppy. However, she realizes that maybe the puppy belongs to someone else. She takes a picture of the puppy. She pastes it on the Board. On top, *written,*

She runs to the road and paste the board. Then go to buy food.

Time passes and no sign of the owner of the puppy. She continues to take care of him. Training him to run. To communicate with her. She gives it a name. **Ai**. She calls him **Ai**. Ai get big each day. He gets used to the house. He knows Mandy as his owner. She takes him out for a walk. They play together in and out of the yard. Ai loves her. *One-day time* comes that she should go set a rose again.

This time she goes with him. Hoping to introduce her to her mom's grave. When they go there, she does the same thing like now and then. This time she also tells her mom that a friend is real. Ai keeps running around the cemetery, she just watches him, and she laughs. At least she has someone to be with around.

Thunder rolls. The lighting flashes. The black cloud comes down. Rains start to drop. Ai, Mandy calls. No sign of Ai. She places hands on her mouth. She hopes to call a little bit louder. She calls, again, yet nothing. She looks around, but only she can see, heavy rain from little bit afar. The more she calls, she starts to lose her voice. She can't compete with the thunder. She stops trying to listen if she can hear Ai barking. But nothing. She starts to worry. She moves along the fence to check maybe Ai is stuck again. She knows it can't be true. Rain is now falling on her, she gets wet. She decides it's better to walk home, though it's raining maybe she will find Ai. The rain hides the tears in her eyes. She cries herself to sleep, because she has no idea where Ai is. What is he doing, cause the rain is becoming very aggressive. *Again* pain, stuck her, like to two Edge sharpen swords *in* the stomach. At least she taught Ai, to always find his way home.

IN THE MORNING, she wakes up, hoping she will see Ai, next to her bed. But nothing. And this really kicks her in her heart. With the thought that she lost her mom. And now her friend is out there in the rain, with no one to help him.

Her *grandpa,* tries to console her. But due to what she's been through, Ai is what she needed. Though grandpa is an old man. He tries to be there for her. Since she's the only one to his daughter. He tries going out with her looking for Ai. But the age and walking with stick. It's better he stays at home. He teaches her to shoot, just incase something happens.

The nights are getting colder. Her lips become numbs. She hides herself in the room.

It's as if I am losing everything I love and care for. First it was mom, and now Ai. Aren't complaining, grandpa is like a father to me. He has been there since mommy went to heaven. Yet there are things I can't talk about with him. There are thing's a girl shares with mom. And with Ai, it's something else. However, with grandpa, old stories, she laughs. Trying to take her pain away. I love his stories. He is a good story-teller. She says as she's approaching him, for another untold story. She is thinking of something that can take her mind off, Ai.

IT'S A WONDERFUL MORNING. Look outside. A warm breeze through the bright side of the house. She wears her sneakers, torn Jean and put in a jacket. She grabs the headset and camera on her side. She thinks, she says" she needs some time alone. Time to herself. She's tired of crying inside the house. After crossing the road.

She sees a group of gangs. Covered with chains, tattoos, just walking towards her. What surprises her, she sees them holding a dog. With the same belt as the one she gave to Ai. She freezes, her feet can't move forward. It's like she's chained with a tree, where she can only just stand there. **Ai**, starts to bark, as he looks at Mandy. The gang's, group kick him, to keep quiet. But as they come close to Mandy, he increases the voice, and wants to run to Mandy. But the Guy, hardly kick him of barking. Now he is barking in a painful note because he is being given hard kicks.

"Hi", says Mandy to the gang. "Who are you? What do you want?" They sound as if they are drunk and been smoking. "I am Mandy", she replies. She comes to Ai. I like your dog. She says with a calm voice. She is shivering, knowing drunk people. She has to be very humble for her sake and Ai. He doesn't have a name. Oh, wow he's great. She brushes his head. She spots, his leg. She sees that scar, that she assumes he got it the day she found him.

She then knew that it's him. But the questions strike in the back of her mind. How can she explain and how can she get him back? Ai, sniffles and lick her. He knows her, and he's feeling that he found his owner. As she looks at him. He looks sick or maybe he has not been eating. I know for sure he is being abused. I see how the guy kicks him. It breaks my heart into pieces.

IN THE NIGHT he comes to her dreams. She feels guilty she couldn't help him. She can't sleep, thinking of what the boys been treating him. Maybe it's even worse than that. He has lost weight too. She tells the story to grandpa. Fortunately, he is known as the retired FBI, so he still has his gun. He promises her that tomorrow morning, they going to go where the gang hang around. Yet the place can be so dangerous, because many stubborn young people roam around. She tries to sleep. At least around 5:30 she was already up. She prepares breakfast for grandpa. After that they grandpa and her hit, his Old truck.

With his Gun on the dashboard.
With his cowboy hat. He drives
off. It's good there's no trafficking
at this ungodly hour.

At the scene the gang become
aggressive to give away the dog.
They claim it belongs to them. Yet,
when they communicate with him,
he never responds. Yet to Mandy
he even shakes his tail. As an
expression of knowing who he is
talking to. Just as grandpa, take on
the gun. The boys did the same.
Unfortunately, they are too many.
Knowing them their conscious is
buried, when they are drunk. One
of the boys let the dog run. One
pulls out the trigger and shot him
on the leg. He screamed, but never
stop running. Grandpa and
Mandy exit the scene. Worry is

back again. Cause they don't know where Ai went.

Grandpa and Mandy hug each other. They get home and sits at the porch. They watch the swing and Mandy is just in grandpa's arms. She rests her head in his chest. As she sobs, for Ai. While they are still sitting, they see Ai, at the front door bleeding so badly. They take him to vet hospital. They checked him, he has lost lot of blood, and he's very weak. But "he's going to be fine", says the doctor, who's helping him. Mandy stands there beside him. Grandpa bring coffee, and at least she feels better.

Hours later, the doctor came to Mandy and grandpa. "Hi, I have good news, you can go home with

Ai, but the bad news is that he has lost his leg. However, it's better animals are able to walk with three if they lose one". At the back of the yard. Mandy built a room

and starts rescuing dogs, that are neglected or either injured. She takes care of them and give them to those who need them and keep others. Though Ai, is now in bad shape, she never gives him away. He's still the best friend she needs.

In her next visit to her mom's grave. Ai, is now able to pick a flower. He carries it with his mouth. They walk to the cemetery. She sometimes run before him, vice versa. He put the white flower on Mandy's mom grave. This time she didn't let any tear to drop, but smile. She comes back, find grandpa on the front step of the house. He smiles as they walk in the yard. In the back you can hear the sound of other dogs playing. She kisses grandpa, and Ai, just, groans, as if he's jealous. Grandpa is so over the moon, that today he sings 'I hope you dance', and he dance with Mandy. Ai never got lost again, and he never let go of Mandy or grandpa.

* My stolen childhood *

The Field is dry. There's no rain, nothing is growing. Yesterday we had the last meal.

There's no money to buy food. There's nothing in the stall, All the cows and goats are gone. Draught brought us poverty. We don't know what we going to eat the next day. My father is just a drinking man. My mother tries to make means ends. My father just get money and take it all to the beer store. When my mom talks sense to him, he is violent. Then one evening he decided to look for a job. When he has no money, he is a good father and a husband. However, no leopard can change his spots. He is untrue to his words. He changes like weather when he has money and he never listen.

He took his suitcase luggage and his pipe on the mouth. His shoes were shining; *you could see your own face if you look closely.* I accompanied him to the bus stop. He Said he was going to look for a job and he will come back to us. He boards in the bus, he sat where I could see him. I waved at him. But dust clouds my eyes, so I could not see the end of the bus. This rocky and dust, with no shoes on my feet. It has always been like these. We can hardly afford food; therefore, this is a minor thing. Many people of my age, we live like this, isn't surprising. Before I could go back home, I passed by my friend's place, so later we can go to play soccer.

On my way home I think of, how the situation is going to be without dad. However, I know she is a strong and beautiful black woman. She put her family first. Though situation is bad at home, she never once, says something about living my dad. She always stays true and hard-working woman. I suppose our grandma taught her well, she endures and persevere, even when it seems unnecessary. I think the African proverb, really got in her, _a woman's grave is in her, in-laws._ She goes to and from collect the wood in the bush. She carries water in her head, with no wheelbarrow. She has been trying to sell few goods, so she can make money. But with the economy that has fallen, it's hard. People can hardly but, and goods just get rotten, until we use them at home or throw away.

ONE DAY, Mama fell to sleep. I waited for her to wake up. It's unusual for her to wake up so late. But then I walk in her room. It was just a beautiful roundel, not far from what we call a kitchen in Africa. It's where I sleep also. It was only three roundels, I have to take a kitchen, cause the other one is for the girls, my three younger sisters.

The clinic is far from here, and there's not even a single cent to pay for a car to take her to the clinic. I just had to run to the bush, and get some medicine, the one's

Grandma taught me about when she was still alive. So, I grill and give my mom, so she can stop coughing. I know it's been a year mountain for her, she needs some rest. But I pray every night, that she gets better. At least this one I learn from her. *"No matter the circumstances she never stops praying"*.

Mama's illness, didn't really get better, but she keeps talking about God. Keeping on praying. I then said to her, "Mama you are sick, and you are still praying. But you are not even healing. Where is that God that you speak of his love, because it's clear his not showing anything here? Daddy left, it's been months he never writes any letter or send money. God knows if he's still alive. I am tired of seeing you like this, it's traumatizing". **Musa**, is very much angry, you could see the agony, in his eyes. His face turns red, as he speaks to his mother. She coughs, as she tries to pick up a cup of water that is besides her. She struggles to sit still on her blankets. Musa helps her to sit. She says, *"Musa, you are still young, but one day you will know, see, and understand that the God I am praying to, He is a living God. And every single tear drops and prayer that I made; he will answer."* She goes back to lay down on her back. Musa, then lay his hand oh her eyes, and he kisses her on her head.

Musa shuts a door with anger. He goes to the girls; they have to go to school. At least it's Friday. They will help with house chores tomorrow morning. It's been long since, I even play soccer game, I miss that place, it's my dream to become a soccer star. Since Mama fell sick, I've been missing every single thing I used to like. I have to go collect woods. Carry water, do laundry, cook at home. And most importantly have to take care of mom, I can't let her die now I still need her and the girls too.

"There is a soccer tournament, on Saturday", Says, *Vusi*. Musa's friend. Yes, I heard, but I am not sure if I will make it. Come on boy, you have to be there, you know that without you the team can't make it. And I haven't been practicing, so the coach won't allow me to play. I have to take care for my family, you know the situation at home. "Okay bra, but if you get the chance, just tag along. Maybe you might be lucky and be selected to play for free stars, the one you like, cause the coach will be selecting today", Says Vusi as he's leaving. The words Vusi said, keeps coming back to his mind. Maybe it's my chance to become a star.

ON SATURDAY MORNING, Musa wake up and do some house chores that girls can't do. He takes food to his mom's room, and everything that she needs daily. Because today he can't be around. He heads to the ground, and sees other's doing some warm up. When the coach sees him. He waves at him, to come warm up with others. Musa, get close, bit nervous, that maybe he doesn't stand a wonderful chance to play today. *"Get dressed boy, today it's going to be a long day. I hope your mama will get well soon"*. That's all he says to him.

Musa's team get in the ground and play their heart off, to ensure that they win the tournament. As the game continues, the opposition team, is leading, and this frustrate, Musa. Because he wants to change his poverty back at home. His father failed the family. The team plays. However, they come second. But for Musa to be picked, it didn't need his team to be number one or in a first team. His skills, talent and determination, gave him the opportunity to be the chosen one. He got the opportunity to go play for free stars. After the game coach, wishes him well, and tap his shoulder, "*you did well son. I know you can go very far with this, all the best*". Musa wipes the sweat with his T-shirt.

While he is going something pops in his mind. He has the opportunity to play for the best team. But he has to leave his family behind. Who will take of them? Many questions pop in his mind, but answers are few. How do I tell them that I am leaving? He sits underneath of the Marula tree. His joy is overshadowed by the pain of going away. But he has a dream to live for, which will also help his younger sisters and mother. Now he is stuck between a hard rock and reality. *"My childhood is stolen, if daddy was there, I would not think twice about this. He left us with nothing, and here I have to be a man, at this age"*. He kicks the tree, as he is furious.

He gets home, he checks on his sister's they are asleep. His mom still awakes. She's waiting for him to come back. He walks in to the room, and sit on the floor. "Boy, what is happening?", Mom' asks him.

Before he can answer, he starts to cry. "Mama I am sorry"; he deeply fell on her legs. Repeatedly, saying I am sorry. "You are freaking me out, son". What happened when you were out? Mom, *"I got picked to play for the free stars"*. Mom smiles, Baby you don't have to be sorry, you have to chase your dreams. I and the girls will be fine. "How Ma, you barely get off these blankets, who will take care of you and the girls?", He says, in so much pain. I promise you that by tomorrow, God will heal me and I will be on my feet again. I will do my best. You are still young; I am sorry it was taken away from you. But now spread your wings and fly.

After three months, Musa has to go. At least his mom is much way better than before. but still Musa is not able to accept that he has to leave his family behind. He packs his luggage. Just few shorts and T-shirts he has. He calls mom into the room, "Mom I am leaving and I promise I will come back to you, and the girls, I won't leave you like the way Dad did". It's ok son, go make me proud. They hug and pass their goodbyes. However, playing for his favorite team, deprived him the chance of finishing his studies. Yet he urges his sisters to hold on, so they can be successful.

The first pay he gets back home. His family is happy to see him. He bought presents for them. Every one of them. They are happy to see him. He tells Mom that the poverty is over and that he is planning on building a house for her. The good news is that; the girls are doing well at school. He asks mom to stop doing all this hard labor, he will send her money every now and then. Musa, visit home, every holiday and When he has time. He saved money to buy all the materials needed to build a five-room house.

A DAY BEFORE CHRISTMAS. While sitting on the veranda, facing the road. A kind man is walking to the house. He looks familiar. But He wait until he says his greetings. In Africa, a lot of man takes Off the hat, when entering home. The man takes off the hat. Only to find that it's my father. He looks nothing. Like the way he left. He's not having a suitcase anymore. His shoes aren't shining. He's just wearing flip flops. He sits on the floor, ignoring the chair. He looks very shy, maybe he's seeing that the house he left is no more. Mom welcome him and never say anything about why he left his family to suffer from hunger, and never come back or at least send money to buy food.

Every time I look at him; I see the moment's I missed as a child. I became man, while he ran off. At least now I know why Mom keep on praying to God. The girls are all studying towards degree of their choice. But today he has no say in anything not because one asks him to be quite. But because of his guiltiness. _**To this**_ day he never speaks of what happened to him when he got there. Mom just thank God that he came back alive. But his true nature is eaten by the prey, and has lost his dignity and respect as a man. When I get married, *"I will never walk out of my kids and wife"*, Musa says, as he falls asleep on his king bed sized.

* When my days are over *

Indeed, there's time for everything, and times happens to everyone; the sun rises, and goes down but the day will never come back. It was Alexa as she tries to meditate on her death bed. She moved her arm to take a cellphone underneath the pillow. The room was full of people who seems to be waiting for their last day, just like she was. She picked phone, unlock, and tried to scroll to see whom she might call, unfortunately there was no one she could think of because they just left the room not long ago.

But instead of mourning she took her Bible and started to read from the first chapter as if she had never read before. The Bible was her only comfort, in the days of distress. Not a day she would question the existence nor the power of God, though she was in her last's days. Though her voice was deteriorating, she always read the Bible and closed her eyes like she was sleeping but she was praying inside. She would always say that she was surrounded by

the angels and that only her flesh
was in pain but the spirit was free
and very much alive.

Some days are better than others, as she
stepped from the bed, it was long-
time after she stepped down. She
looked around just to see many
people from both ages, lying in
their beds. She asked for a sip of
water, and she could preach to
them about the Love of Christ.
Even the visitors could listen to
her as she spoke like someone
who was not sick, but she could
sometimes cough. She told them
that Christ was everything and
sickness only affected the flesh,
but the spirit is string and that
what matters most. People who
came to see their loved ones,
though they were troubled, they

would return home in peace after she spoke.

SUNDAY MORNINGS was different from other days, Alexa's sickness was escalating, the doctors called her home and many of her relatives came as they received news. Doctors were trying to do everything in their power to make the situation better, though she stopped them, told them to leave her in peace. The doctors found that her cancer has now spreading more than before and that her days were very few. People gathered around her bed, with a bunch of bouquet, and they tried to comfort her that it's going to be fine, she looked at them and said I am fine. People looked shocked and other cried as she said those

words, and thinking of what the
doctors said *"about her days being
numbered"*.

While in front of everyone she
opened the Bible and she read in
the book of John, then prayed, and
tried to speak up but her voice
was no longer strong enough. She
opened eyes and asked, "why
though cry for me? Don't you
know that I am fine, I am not
alone. Cry for your souls, my soul
is in the father, have you accepted
Jesus Christ? I have and I am not
afraid of death, for Jesus
conquered. And the number of my
days. You've seen me, preached
the gospel, everywhere I walked, I
devoted my life to him and tell
you what the Lord has been and

always with me, I've seen him and his glorious Grace, and here in this bed, he still worthy to be worshipped therefore, I do, like I did".

She felt the strong wave and sat up in her bed, and everyone was amazed of what happened, she told them the angel gave her the strength. As people saw what happened to her, they asked *"where was this God?"* she preached to them by opening the book of John 3:16, and how his love is for everyone. And many wanted to have the faith she had even when she was in pain. She prayed for many souls, and said they would be immersed when they go back home, and live their lives for Christ.

After preaching she was again weak, and she opened her mouth to say, "when my days are over, I would be glad because I know I will go to my Fathers; God and the son, he who have brought me here want me back. When my days are over, I will rejoice because I've done his Will in good and bad times, and what I feel now will soon be over" She asked for rest for a moment, unfortunately it was the end of her on earth, but new day in heaven, however little did they knew that she was gone. They just sat there as rehearsed of what she told them. Until when the doctors came in and declared her dead.

She was taken from the hospital and laid to rest in her home behind her house.

* We all want out *

"Hello, is anyone at home?" , Asked John as he opens the kitchen door. No one is in here. "Baby? Cindy?" But there was no reply. John went to the bedroom and threw himself on the bed, and stretched out his hand. He was feeling tired it was a long day. With endless meetings. He worked at a CC company and he was the CEO for over 10 years. He has achieved everything and he had money with good wife, and a fancy mansion with different cars, yes, he was successful. John took the phone and call Cindy, "hi?"

Cindy's voice on the voicecall. "Hey baby, where are you?", asked John? "Oh, I am sorry I went to the dentist, but I am already on the drive way".

John slept like a baby, on the bed, "hey?" Said Cindy as she speaks to John. But he couldn't move a bit, until she touched him and he wake up. "hey, I was thinking that maybe today we can just go out for dinner, me and you alone at our favorite restaurant". Well as john stands up and draw nigh next to Cindy, "mm what a thoughtful idea, but babe?", before he can finish, she, was like ag, here we go again, please, arh when is the last time we went out or at least be romantic? John, "whoa, sh, I have a better idea, why don't you join me in the shower and after we will cook together and have the best dinner ever after".

The following day they both went to work, and when they come back, they sat down, and John said babe, "you know I love you right?", Cindy yes and you know I do too? Replied John of course. Where is this coming from Cindy asked? John scratched his hand, and could not find words on how to say anything, please don't take this the wrong way, I don't want to hurt you. Cindy, yeah sure its ok. You can talk to me we've been married for a long time; you know me. He took her hands and hold them tight, he said to her, "you are a beautiful and intelligent woman, your smart, and I like your independence, you're the strongest woman I've ever met, and you've been there for me all the way from kindergarten, and I love you, and forever grateful". Asked Cindy where are you going with all this talk? *"I am saying that I love you, let me take a shower we will talk next time".*

Cindy couldn't get what John said off her mind, and every time she brought the conversation, he would just say it was nothing. Their relationship was a roller coaster. They have been married out of love, based on culture, and they stayed together and respected their culture. However, as time goes by, as they explore other cultures and meet different people, they realized that some people married for love and they stayed happily ever after, though it also happens in arranged marriage. Their families wanted them to be together, as they've known each other for a long time, and their families are friends, so it was good for a marriage. But the two started to grow apart in their marriage, and they stayed because they didn't want to disappoint their families. But every day they knew that they both wanted out.

"Hi, I am doing good thanks, how are you?" it was Cindy on the Phone call outside the porch. She was talking to Hamilton, the dentist. John came and stood behind her, without talking, and she didn't see her. She sounded so happy on the phone, and she was LOL, talking about the times they spent together, and that she enjoyed every moment with him. At the end of the call she said *"I love you too*". As she looked behind her, she saw John with hand on his pocket. "How long have you been standing here?" Asked Cindy. *"Don't worry long enough to know that you love him? Who is he?"* Its Hamilton the dentist. Oh, John went to watch the TV, and Cindy just stood for a while and then she followed him, "can we please talk?", Ask Cindy. Well let's go outside under the moon, said John.

They sat on the porch and watched the stars and moon, with the whisky added ice, and play their song that they first danced to. "You don't have to worry", said John, I know that our marriage was not the best one to put on history of love, we only did it because we had no choice. Do you remember that day when I said I love you and how beautiful you were? She nodded. That day I realized that there was someone making you happy and I was not the one. And I really want you to be happy and feel what love is, *love is a beautiful thing in the world, and if it come your way, take it, appreciate it;* me and you we are just the cult of our traditions, and that always made us unhappy. But before I say more, I want to ask you a question? "Sure, you can ask me anything and I will answer honestly", said Cindy. "Do you love him? Does he make you happy?" She sighed, I love him, and I am happy when I am with him, and I will always love you too. He smiled and kissed her forehead and say I am happy for you.

"John wake up, it's time to go to work", said Cindy. Ouch! "hey, I am taking a day off today".

No, you can't do that, you've never done that, why now? I want to spend this day with you. well really that is ok I'd love that too. Its ok. It was during launch when John said, I have a confession too, I haven't been really good husband, I also found someone, and I loved her like you do to Hamilton, and don't you worry about our parents we will talk to them and tomorrow I will meet up with my lawyers so that we can file divorce papers. I would also like to meet this guy who stole

you away from me, and they both
laughed.

It was Friday evening, and John called
for a family gathering, both his
and her wife's parents for a
Saturday night. "Hey, Cindy you
know what, the way our parents
don't know what we are up to, I
am so happy. Gee stop it. This is
not funny, they going to kill us
today". Cindy stopped and looked
John on his face, and I am proud
of you and I love you so much,
and what you're doing for us is
very much important and not only
to us, but the next generation too.
Its brave. And hey before our
parents bring tears to us, let me
say this, you know you will
always be the important part of
my life, and I wish you all the best

in your future endeavors, be the happiest man ever. They hugged each other and burst into tears, and they sat on the sofa, and talked all night long, and enjoyed each other's' companion.

SATURDAY MORNING, they were both excited of the biggest days, however it was not going to end well between their families, but they had to do it, get out of there. They prepared their traditional and western food all the drinks were served, and family members were arriving. After all members have arrived, they sat and talked, and laughed and enjoy food on the table. Then john coughed a little, and held Cindy's hand and wipe his mouth with napkin. He thanked everyone that came that day, he said, "we called you here today because, me and Cindy sat down and talked about it and we came to conclusion that", John's mom interfered before he could finish, "yes! my son we've been waiting for so long to have grandkids, thanks", as they all smiles.

"Please Ma let me finish", As I was saying we decides to have divorce and the lawyer is working on it, we are going separate ways, we were never happy since day one in this marriage, we were just friends not good for marriage, and we both want to marry people we love, we don't want to add another statistics number for arranged, forced, and unhappy marriages. We both happy with our decision. Its mutual, before we break each other's hearts. We are divorcing!

* Love or money *

It's been half a decade since Mary been with Randle. No one could ever separate them, they loved each other and everyone could see that. She was a successful manager in one of the Worldwide companies, known to make lot of money. And even she was earning well, she managed to build a house for her parents' back home in the village and took care of her siblings. Though she moved to the city, she never forget her way back home to her family.

Mary and Randle spent time together on holidays they even paid for vacations overseas. Together they seemed happy and things were going well between them, in general. It was **<u>Sat morning</u>** when Mary decided to do a spring cleaning. It's been long since she did that, as her career kept her busy and working late at some point. The music kept her company as she was moving all the cupboards in the absent of Randle, who is known to have gone to a meeting. Mary knew that every Sat Randle was never around, and it never bothered her, as she knew he was a working man.

As she was unpacking Randle T-Shirts, she came across an

engagement ring, and hello! she jumped in the house like a horse in a competition towards the winning point. In her mind she, was like, Yes, it's time, she had been waiting for all along. "When was he going to pop the question, duh? Its every girl's dream" From that moment cleaning was so exciting and very quick, with few dances at some point. she put the ring back to where it was and promised herself that she will pretend as if she saw nothing. The sun went down and time for Randle to come back was drawing near. She then decided that she would prepare a romantic dinner for two.

The car was on the driver way, when Mary looked through the window and saw Randle. She kept smiling over and over again,

she hoped to spice things so that maybe Randle would then propose that day. However, her point was not to rush him, but to show him that love was still alive between them. Randle parked the car, and as soon he stepped down, he called, "Baby!" She went back fast and throw herself on bed, with some lingerie, one of Randle's favorite. She laid on her side as if she was in photo-shooting for magazine. Randle opened the door to be welcomed by the roses that lead him to their bedroom. Randle, *"mm, today seem like I'm the lucky guy"*, He said. She played Marvin Gaye song *Sexual *healing**, damn, who could resist that?

He took off his jacket and tie, drew closer to the bed, on the bottom and ran his hand from her legs to the breast. She looked at him and together they smiled. Slowly he climbed the bed and kissed her body gently and very smoothly. *"I love you"*. Randle whispered, can I have your lips, it was just rhetorical, they kissed each other. After they were done making love, they went to take bath and had a peaceful night. However, that did not make Randle ask her to marry him, she just believed that maybe he was not ready he still needed some time. Mary kept hoping that the day would come, though she never knew when, it was like chasing the shadow of yourself.

DAYS WENT BY, still nothing and Randle never talked about marriage, and every time she brought the topic, he just changed the subject. No matter how she tried, she kept failing. Though he never spoke of it, it never gave her any doubts about him, as he was always home on time, and nor his phone was she not allowed to pick it up or check texts messages, except for Sat where he always had a long meeting. But that was not a big deal, Randle kept doing what he used to do since the day they met, and rekindle their love now and then. They went for vacations and celebrate each and

every inch of their anniversary,
nothing odd he ever done.

One time, Mary with girl's night and
Randle decided that he had lot of
work to do and meet the
deadlines. So, she left him, and she
was not bothered that something
might happen on her absent. She
went to camp, and her friends
celebrated on her arrival. Things
with the girls only, they do things
they can't in front of men. And
everything was fine, happy
moments. She and Randle call
each other every day and that
gave Mary assurance that she was
the only lady in his life. But deep
in her heart she was worried, why
it is taking him so long to ask,
after she had seen the ring.

In the afternoon in a restaurant, the girls were sitting and having time of their lives, Mary and her friends back home. And suddenly the topic popped, about the engagement ring in the closet. As the drinks were coming on and on, and talking became more intense, **Cecil**, mistakenly said, 'Randle has another woman'. "What?" Mary asked? "hey Mary come on, everyone knows here in the office, they are always clinging on each other's lap". Mary took off the cup of wine that Cecil was holding and put it down, "what do you mean he has a lady?" Asked Mary. Ok, said Cecil, it true why would I lie to you, I have nothing to gain by telling lies nor nothing to lose by speaking the truth. Mary as she was still shocked, did you guys know about this? Asked the other group of friends, and with shame they bent their head downwards, and said yes. She walked away, as if she wanted fresh air, on the outside of the restaurant on a cold winter.

When the *evening came*, Mary decided it was time to go home, and she got in the car and went home without saying a word to her friends. She cried all the way home, sobbing while driving, she did not even understand what was going on her mind. She got home and the house was empty, she went to the sofa and laid there for a moment. Later she woke up and went to clean herself, she did not want Randle to see her like that, she didn't even know what to say to him. Randle never came home because he thought the camp was going to take a week.

MONDAY EVENING, Randle came back home, for he knew she would be home too by then. Like usual the conversation went well and all the pretense prevail from Mary. The situation was eating her day by day, and she had no strength to confront him, or maybe she was afraid of losing him, maybe she would be pushing him straight to her arms. In the process of pretense, she was slowly growing anger and losing her true self and growing distant from Randle. She realized how broken she was becoming and hurting she was feeling and not be able to express it, the betrayal to those she called friends and the one she called her man.

Every time she looked in the mirror, she saw someone, she never met, that happy and in love lady was, like an old woman who had seen it all and the loses. What bothered her was that Randle was the same man, he never asked anything on anyway, it was all normal for him. And that made her more rage as she felt like he was less caring, as he seemed to never ask if things were ok with her. Mary waited for Randle to come back the other night, and she felt ready to confront him, and she went to take the ring, only to find that it was misplaced from where it was. Many questions popped in her head, "did he proposed to her chick, what might have happened?" So many questions but with no answers.

After months Randle came home, and said he had something to talk to her. They sat down. He went down on her knees and held the hand and they locked eyes. Randle spoke these words, "you know I love you, and I could never love anyone the way I love you, and no matter what happens I want you to promise that you will still love me through it all, because you are my best friend, and we've known each other from kindergarten and from then our love has never went cold". As she was responding, **"I love you"**, Randle interrupted, please let me finish, "*I am getting married and I want you to be there on* *the wedding ceremony, please come because I love you, I can't do this without you*". she shook off her hand, and stood up and walked away, she only said "if you loved me, I would be the one you were marrying so it's clearly not me since the ring that was in the closet underneath the black shirt, you bought is no longer there. I wonder what kind of love is this after years of being stuck with you wasting my time". She went to the room and locked the door, cried so bitterly. Randle begged her to open and she could not, the next day she skipped going to work and packed her clothes and went home to her family for love and comfort.

Randle _got married_ and she saw pictures on social media, and they even went to the place where she hoped her honeymoon would be. And that was all gone taken away from her and her world just crumbled. It took time for her to try and live a better life without him, she would remember everything and cried all alone, however, that did not change anything but just made situation worse as she was always indoors trying to mend her broken hearted. She went back to work after she took a leave, and during lunch she would remain in her office while other went out. She became a loner and wanted nothing to do with anyone.

<u>*The time goes by*</u> and she was getting better and recovering and Martin was her shoulder when she was feeling sad. Miracles does happen; from being a shoulder that grew stronger day by day, that lead to romantic love. **Martin** never wasted his time with a wonderful respectful and loving Mary, and any man would be lucky to have her. After six months of dating he asked her to marry him and they got married, went to Paris; city of Love, for honeymoon. Together they bought house in Atlanta and had two kids, Son Lucas and Daughter, Alexa and they lived happily ever after. And hey, the fact that Martin was Randle best friend never occurred in any day of their lives, they loved each other.

One day on the internet Mary came
across the news that Randle was
divorced and he lost everything to
her including the house, and the
woman went further to post on
her Instagram page that '*some
things we only do for money, e.g.
marry, and put a smiley face.* I
pray that he become happy again.

* My beloved sister *

I had no idea what to do at such age.
I was very young. So was my
sister. Our parents got divorced.
My mother left us with my father.
For few months he stayed with us.
Only one day to wake up with my

sister without parents. Where my mother went, remained mystery. My father married another wife. He tried to be there for us. But it changed because my aunt could not raise us. We were not her children. That she made it clear. She always told us that your mother left, because she doesn't love you, because you are bad children. And she is not coming back to take you. After a year My father left to live with my aunt in her house. He left us with nothing. To raise each other. To love and care for each other.

WHEN THE NIGHT CAME. I kept looking at the roof. A roof that let the moon light inside. It kept me from sleeping for most of the years. As it rained, it poured inside the house. Clothes would be wet, and sometimes it rained for few days. The words my aunt said to us, always came to my mind. "You are bad children", our mother doesn't love us. Every night I and my sister slept in fear of what might happen to us. But I always knew that _he that keeps Israel never sleep no slumber._ At times we had no food, because I was still young. Unless I go out on the streets to beg, and picked on the waste bins. We then had no food.

Our neighbors laughed us; they could not help. They stood by the fences and throw left overs. I would run and picked them. Some were even rotten. We were like dogs. With no hope. My sister was very young. I was just a boy I didn't know what to with a young girl. Sometimes, I would cry, when I looked at her. I knew she needed a mother. Or rather a female figure. Crying was not going to make change. I had to be a brother and a mother at the same time. So that I could take care of *Sana*. I had to make sure she was fed. With the little I would get. I would rather sleep on an empty stomach while she was full. I protected her, against all odds.

God does answers prayers. And he heard me when I prayed. A social worker organized adoption for me and Sana. The unfortunate part was that we had to go separate ways. Because the families that was supposed to adopt us where different. On my last day with Sana. I told her, I promised her that when my time comes, I would look for her and we will be together again. She was young, she couldn't understand what was happening. Our mother left, when she was just nine months. She could barely remember her, if she were to come back. My prayer was that; wherever she was going, may they really take care of her. I loved Sana with all my heart. She was the only one left. When everyone packed and walked from us.

When I got to my adoptive parents. My first month was like hell. I had to live without Sana. I knew, I was happy. I was in a safe place. The *Jacksons* family were very much good to me. I always wished Sana could be with me. She was part of me that I could never trade for anything. At night I prayed that God protects her. The only time I saw the moon was when I was outside. It reminded me of Sana. Sometimes I would just go out purposefully, just to watch it. I would communicate with it, like it was Sana. When it rained, I believe that it was not raining on her. I loved her. She was my blood. Those months I spent it with less communication, to the Jacksons family.

I accepted that I will always be, *Marvin*, Sana's brother. But I had to be living and be Jacksons son. I found myself a brother, only two years older than me. ***Lionel***. Lionel was a good brother I could ever ask for. He was raised well-mannered by his parents. He listened to them, and had a respect for them. I never wished I was born in the Jacksons, because I knew that I belongs there. God made a way, that was hard to understand when I was young. But finally, I went through it. Lionel would play with me, taught me English. He was very patient with me. I never wanted to disappoint him. I observed the way he lived his love at home. I then lived it, because I wanted to be a good kid in the Jacksons. It was simple because it was a good way of living. Happy family. Full of respect for both young and old. Mostly full of love. But My love was still for Sana.

What I loved about the Jacksons was that. Instead of providing food for someone. I was being provided for. Not that I complained. I was a child, who have parents. Though I loved the Jacksons, my love for Sana, was still like fire flames. The Jackson signed up for me to go to school. I was already behind. But Lionel has taught me, what I needed for that period. He helped me to study. He was basically my mentor. And I loved him. I tried my best in class, in the end I passed with good grades. Indeed, Lionel was a great teacher and mentor to me. He would see my results and applause me. Every little achievement was celebrated in the Jackson. We were all celebrating, because Lionel and I were top achievers. After a school, we did home chores and cleaned the garden. After writing homework.

One thing that I nearly, experienced was some foolish hatred from other boys. They would laugh at me, when I was walking. Only because my color of skin was different from theirs. But that didn't bother me. Because when the Jacksons looked at me, they saw Lionel's young brother. And that all I could ever ask. Lionel would discipline them. Whenever we were walking if they started racist comments. He would just go to them and put his hand, on my shoulder. He told them I was his brother. He loved me for who I am. And that we were all human, created by God. The only difference we had in the Bible was language. We are born of God. He would just say that and we walk. They never repeated again.

Two days before Lionel's birthday. We were all preparing for the day and very happy. It seemed like it was a norm, to celebrate in that side of the country. Cause even on his parent's birthdays, we celebrated. Mrs., Jackson, she asked me when was my birthday. She was so humble. Down to earth. She spoke in a well soft voice. She always smiles after speaking. She was very beautiful. Most of all full of kindness. Though I and Lionel did something wrong. She would talk to us as if she was praising us. From that moment I knew, where Lionel got his character. I told them my birthday was three days ago. Prior to Lionel's. She insisted that I should have told her. I didn't because where I come from, I never celebrated a birthday. I didn't know that we had to. "You should have told me", she said. But instead we celebrated Lionel's and mine though it had already passed.

I graduated and with the Grace of God I got job. A job Lionel helped me find. Worked as an IT. I've always loved it. Though Lionel, moved out of the house. He would still visit us in the home. And we had a wonderful time at his presence. It's **been years** since I saw Sana. I promised to look for her until I find her. I thought in my mind. My heart never forgotten about her. I told the Jacksons family about her, because they didn't know. I kept it to myself all those times. And I felt bad about it. I apologized to the Jacksons. Lionel assured me that we would find her. And we would be reunited again. As an IT practice I had a clue Where to start looking for her. With a privilege of social media. It was my first choice.

After some time of many attempt with no luck. Lionel, came with the information that may lead to her whereabouts. We took a way down to, **George**. Where we hoped to find her. When we asked in the neighborhood, the name of Sana was something new to them. We parked a car outside the road. We sat, I was sweating and even tired. I saw someone walking towards the car, where we parked. Lionel said, a lady coming looked very fine and beautiful even from far. I slowly got off the car seat, I opened the door. I knew it was long since I saw her, 25 years ago. But my eyes could never have missed Sana. I knew she couldn't recognize me; I was a man. I talked to her. I called her Sana. She looked at me and fly straight to my arms. She knew that no one ever called her that except me her brother. My beloved sister I found her like I promised.

The only reason, Sana was unknown was because she changed name. Her adoptive parents made her change her names. But that didn't

bother me. I was so pleased that I
found her. They raised her well.
She told me she had an amazing
childhood after we left home. We
travelled back from George. We
got home with the Jacksons
together with Sana's adoptive
parents. We had an amazing and
unforgettable moments of
celebration. Every day I thank
God for the parents He gave us.
With the Jacksons I never felt
anything more than just their
second born. As for our biological
parents. We just wished then the
best wherever they are. Maybe we
would have found them if we
looked for them.

Sana and Lionel got married.
Strengthening the family Bond to
be never broken. I knew Lionel

was a good man. He would take care of My Sana. I loved her. On their wedding day I didn't know whether to be the best man or walk her down the Aisle. But I let Sana's father to took the position. I was the best man. I knew they would live a happily life. I am Jacksons son, a brother to Sana, Marvin.

* The loss of my innocence *

"Woman open this door, before I break it down".

"Please my husband stops this, it's early for shouting in the morning", says Lizzy, as she takes off the blanket. The kids are still sleeping, they have to wake up soon and get ready for school. How many times must I tell you, Paul! Your daughter is not supposed to be at school, only, Barry can go. "Mom what's going on?" Asks Indiana. Please go to sleep my flower, respond Lizzy, to Indiana. It's okay sleep, I will wake you up soon. *My husband please keep it low; I don't want our neighbors coming asking what's happening here in the morning*". Just take your food in the microwave and eat. I'm drunk I don't want any food, where is my son, Barry.? Don't make a sound he is asleep; you will see him in few hours. No! Paul pushing Lizzy to hit the headboard. Barry, Daddy is here wake up. My husband he is too tired, please leave him to sleep.

Eish, Lizzy's voice, standing in front of the window. "Mon what happened?", ask Indiana. It's nothing, my angel, go take a shower. But mom, you're hurt, and looks like you were bleeding. Lizzy stop looking at the mirror, my angel, I promise you it's nothing, I just hurt myself yesterday, when I was, you know, it's ok. Are you sure Mom? asks Indiana, with eyes that says worried, painted all over her face. Yes, let me wake your brother while you finish, hurry up before the school bus leaves you behind. Ok mom. Paul, "where is my Keys, I put them here yesterday?" My husband I haven't seen them, since I woke up, she responding while getting Barry out of bed. He is still sleepy though. Hey Barry, the sun is rising, you should really stop watching TV, you see what it's doing to you now. "Lizzy, I asked for my Keys", I'm coming my husband, she smiles and walk with Barry.

LATER after the kids went to school. "Lizzy?" Paul calls, he is now very sober and quiet. Here I am my husband. "My love I just want to apologize for what happened this morning, it wasn't my intention to hurt you, or make noise to the kids". It's ok, Lizzy replies and walks to the kitchen. Here is your lunch box. "Lizzy, I mean it; I am genuinely sorry". My husband I know, it's fine, don't worry. "And anyway, I have been meaning to talk to you about something. Please my dear, take a seat" Paul talking as he sips his coffee. Talk to me, I'm listening, So the thing is that I got a work, job, I don't know really, but I will be earning money. "A job, that's wonderful news I guess, but what kind of job?" Well, she taps her hairs backwards, a house cleaner. What? What do you mean a cleaner, who will take care of your daughter? You mean my kids? Of course, I'm sorry. I am taking this job because of them, and you don't have to remind me now and then that angel isn't yours. Can we talk about this When I get back? Sure.

"Daddy", says Barry running to Paul arms, "My son your back from school? How was your day, what did you do at school?" Indiana, comes in before Barry can answers, "Hello Dad", Indiana, taking off school bag, throwing it to the table. Barry here is food. *"Where is Indiana's plate, Dad?"* Barry asks. Well her Mom will give her when she comes back, and yet she must clean first like her Mama. Barry steps out of his father's arms, and take two slices to Indiana. "Thank you", says Indiana. Barry come here. He walks out with him, holding his hand and pushing him to hurry. Indiana, remains in the room, and eat her brother's sandwich that he shared with her.

"Did you guys write your homework?" Yes, I did, Barry replies with excitation and his lighting eyes, yes, I did mom. That's my boy, good job. Indiana what about you? You have been so quiet ever since I got here, it's unlike you, are you having fever what's the matter? I will write tomorrow in the afternoon mom. It's Saturday. My angel I know, but you always do it on Friday? I know Mom, I want to sleep please. Okay angel. Barry is already asleep, no mama I'm awake, where is Dad? is he coming back? Yes, dear He might be on his way by now. Pray and go to sleep, I love you all. But this time Indiana, just cover herself inside blanket. Barry, what happened at school today? Why is Indiana acting this way? I don't know, she was okay when we came back, and I even shared my bread with her, because she is my sister. What do you mean? When you say you shared bread with her? What about her own? Dad refused to give her, so I gave her some. Oh! God this husband of mine, My God what is happening with me. She turns to Indiana who is not saying any words, I'm sorry my angel about this, it will never happen again.

IT IS SATURDAY MORNING, after Paul got off to the saloon. Like he always does every weekend. He keeps drinking and come home to cause havoc, except for Barry. Lizzy, is in behind the house doing laundry. Can I ask you a question? A voice from the other side, it's Indiana, as she stands behind the tree that gives shadow during summer. You can ask anything my angel I am your mother, Lizzy, stand up straight to look where Indiana is standing. Why Dad hates me so much? I mean mom he loves Barry more, she sits down on the dust, with a long face. Oh, my angel, he does not hate you. He just has his own ways of showing it. Mom every time when you are not around, he has his crazy ways, to a point of denying me food, what kind of love is that. Come here my angel. Don't cry baby. You know I love you right.

Please don't do this to me. I am sorry. Don't hurt me. I am begging you, stop please Sir. A cry and nervousness that no one could ignore. Be quiet, don't make noise or I will silence you for good. Now the sounds are very low, like there's a pillow on her mouth or rather knife on the neck. Indiana, never tell anyone about this, it's between you and I. Don't tell your mama or Barry. Not even your friends. Indiana, her dress, down. It's blood top down the dress. Tears keep falling like rain. She is not even trying to dry them off. As she looks at the door. Her eyes meet with Barry's. Paul as he jumps off the bed. Buttoning his pants. He also sees, Barry. Who just stand silently leaning on the door frame. Barry, how long have you been standing there.? Seeing his sister crying, he cries, without replying to Paul.

Maybe he understands what's happening.

Indiana, what's going on my angel? What happened to the baby I know? You just lock yourself in the house. It's like you're living in your own world. I even hear that your marks are decreasing by day. Your teacher called me. Baby you can tell me. Talk to your mom. It's nothing much I've just been not feeling well. Maybe it's flu. I will take you to clinic tomorrow., Says Lizzy who looks very concerned, because everything is changing, even Barry is no longer a bubbly boy I once knew. Even around the yard you don't play together anymore. We will play Ma, says Barry, as he looks at Indiana. Who sits and cover her legs, so maybe her mom can't see anything. But deep down her world is crumbling. Everything is falling apart. Her innocence is broken, never again to mended.

It's me, Lizzy. She talks to Paul who is beaten up from the sheeben. Thank you, Lizzy. He holds her hand; you are so kind and loving. I do not deserve you. Shh, just take your medication and get some rest, you are very injured. He looks at her as she pours water in an electric kettle. She makes him warm chocolate tea. She grabs the chair and sits next to him. She prays for him. You will get better my husband. "With you by my side of course I will. But Lizzy I have something to tell you". Mom, Indiana walks in. Interrupting, the conversation between her parents. Indiana looks eyes with her Dad, who sighs, as if he is feeling pain. What is it my angel? Asks Lizzy. It's okay, I will talk to you later.

Have you noticed? What, noticed what? What do you mean? I mean Indiana she is do different these days'. She is no longer herself. *"No I haven't she's just*

growing, she needs space. Let her be".
He is shaking as he talks. Avoiding to say
more than he has to. I'm her mother she
should be able to talk to me. I know Lizzy,
let go of it. He breath heavily. The sweat
on his face. Okay fine calm down. I'm just
worried about her. Sorry. I am the one
who should apologize. I understand your
concerns. You love her and you should
be worried. Yes. Anyway, you wanted to
say something before Indiana came in.
Oh yah, it's nothing much I will tell you
when I feel better. Let me rest, he turns
to the other side of the bed. Guiltiness
eats him every day. Yet the courage to
tell the truth he lacks. Death wish
becomes better, when reality seems to
be against you.

You have a high temperature my husband.
How are you feeling? Lizzy I am not
getting any better. Everyday it's a battle.
My mind is tired. I feel like I have a load

of sand on my shoulder. Lizzy, I know I am a drinker. My actions when I'm drunk are out of control. I hurt you and your kids. I know there's is no excuse for what I have done. But unless I tell you this, I won't be free, and the kids. I want you to call the police before I can tell you. What do you mean? My husband? What precisely are you talking about? I am getting scared and confused at the same time. Calm down. Just do as I requested. I also want the kids to be here too. I owe them that much. Okay, let me call the police. But my husband you should tell me first. No, immediately answers Paul. Having been married to you for more than a decade. I know you will try to protect me. It's done. I want to do this the right way.

"I'm glad or scared that you are all here", Says Paul. Looking at Indiana, he holds back tears. She stands, behind her mama. She is somehow anxious. Please all of you listen to me until I'm done talking. And so, you know I'm ready for anything. Lizzy, you love me I know that. I tried to be a better man for you. Yet I have failed every day. But you never forsaken me, you stand by me always. And now I want to be a better person for me. I have hurt you and everyone around me. I can't blame it on alcohol, it's foolishness I know. I get drunk and comes home. Only to wake you up and the kids. I even lay my hands on you, without any cause. You get serious injuries from my beatings. The next day I apologies and promise to never repeat. But its like a song with no melody. I do the same thing from time to time. Honestly you don't deserve any of that. I am truly sorry for everything. I can't say how many times I have abused you since we got married. You are better off without me. You deserve someone better than me, someone kind and generous like you are. And you have been so good to me. You never raised your voice to me.

Everyone, is just so quiet. Says one of the police. Trying to break that silence. Lizzy just stands with her hand on her face. The other one on Indiana's shoulder. Her eyes just stare at him. Indiana? Paul looking at her. A tear falls down from his one eye. "I am and will forever be sorry. I will never be able to forgive myself for what I have done to you. You take me as your father and it's what I should have been. Like I promised your Mama, when she says there's is you. But that day, when I pull your dress on top of your head. You cried for help. But I ignored you. I keep seeing blood on your dress everyday I close my eyes. Barry, you are just young. I understand you couldn't help your sister. But I should not have done that at all", Paul get off bed. He takes his hands on his back. For the police to handcuff him.

Is it because he is not my father? Why Mom? I am lost. He took everything in me. That night you left me and Barry. I will never forget it. Only a day, it's what it takes. It's been months but it feels like it happened today. I can't wash away what he did to me. I live with it. My angel, you know I had no idea he was going to do that. Angel mom, I'm no angel. I'm broken, all is gone. I am sorry Indiana. "Ma, I still have nightmares from that day. Maybe one day I will get better but, the loss of my innocence breaks me into two". Barry just listens as they talk. Paul, is still in jail for a rape case. No one has ever visited him since he was arrested.

* IT LIGHTS AGAIN FOR ME *

IT'S WINTER MORNING. And the snow is falling like rain. The sun will not set, not anytime soon. The mist is everywhere. I can even see it from the mountain. Those trees, with green leaves; they are hidden. The sounds of car hooter. A huge traffic in the lanes. Everyone is busy, rushing to different places. The coldness in my back. I try so hard to cover myself. But no matter how I tried, it's just so cold. I am just seating at the bus stop. I am wearing my favourite red jacket. The jacket my aunt gave to me. This is the one I wear often. The one I have and love most. I am just wearing flip flops, in this aggressive coldness. It's like my feet is inside the snow. Not many people on the streets. I guess it's probably, because they are driving cars. Rather using public transport. Only people I can see is some homeless man. He is just sleeping on the boxes. I know there isn't much I can do for him. I am just a girl from the village. Life is still tough at home. I am waiting for my uncle, who promised to take me to a job interview.

As I am sitting down. My heart and spirit are moved, when I see the man lying outside in this weather. A weather in which people are running away from. I look around to see if my uncle's car is approaching. Gosh, it's just a waste of time. It's all white. I want to make sure that he doesn't pass me. This interview, I have vested my hope in. And I have to get this job. I go, to the man. He is still sleeping. It doesn't feel like he is outside. I guess he has been there for a long time. I shake him. he opens his eyes and looks at me. "What's up?", He asks me. In fear my vocal cracks. I don't even know what to say. I should have thought of it before; I came to him. After few seconds, "Hi, I am Violet", I reply. I just want to know you better. I roll my eyes. I mean of course, it is weird. But yes, I have to. "Why?", He asks me. It doesn't sound like he asked me "why". I honestly don't have many words in me. My words are chewed. and I think I have swallowed them. Fortunately, I hear the hooter. It's my uncle. Goodbye sir. I will see you next time. I run to the car.

Uncle, it's me, getting inside while closing the door. He greets me. "Are you ready?", He asks me. well I am ready. This is my opportunity; I have to do my best uncle. I smile at him. He is looking at the mirror. He smiles back. "I *am proud of you my sister's daughter"* I know you are going to do well. Don't be nervous, trust and believe in God. He encourages me, with every word that I honestly needed to hear. You're smart and intelligent, I wish my brother lived enough to see you. He tells me, and breath out. His smiles wipe out. He loved my father. He was devastated by his passing. I know uncle, but it's all the Will of God, I respond to him. "I don't want to be emotional right now uncle", I say, we all burst into laughter. Here we are, go and do your best. He fixes my red jacket, and my afro hair. I am not going to be able to pick you up after you are done. Take a taxi fare. He hands me, a paper note. I am shy to look at it. I just place it in my red jacket pocket. The one next to my waist.

This day keeps getting better. I say that smiling. Because I am so rest assured that I have the job. I thank God, for all this. Yet there is one thing that keeps coming back again and again. The man I saw in the morning. I think I have time to go to see him again. I check my watch to see what time it is. It's still early. 10:30 in the morning. I will take 11:00 bus. After waiting for roughly 30 minutes. In this cold weather. At least now people are walking in the road. Others are selling in the markets. You can see the coal burning. Woods, as they bake. Its noisy as people shout for various reasons. I finally get in the bus. I sit next to the window. Where I can see outside. I lay my head on the window. I keep brushing off the fog, so I can see clearly. My hands back to the jacket. Outside, I can see bushes, green trees, and beautiful grass. I reach my stop. I get off the bus. After few people, who have been before me.

I look for a place where I saw the man in the morning. I can see him. He is eating. I guess he got himself food. I walk to him. Still nervous again. He looks at me. "Woman, what do you want?", He asks me. I whispers it's me Violet, I talked to you in the morning. I know, I remember you. That's why I am asking, "What is it that you want?", He asks again. In me, I absolutely have no answer sir. I think it's just fate. "Fate, what do you mean?", I put my bag down. Sir I just want to know you better. Again, I fail to respond to his question. I am just a woman from the village. Don't be scared of me. I am not going to do anything harmful. I hand him, a banana that I just bought. I was feeling a bit of hunger. What is your name sir? "My name?". he puffs. My mane is **Herman**. Thank you for telling me. I have to go now. I will see you next time. "Oh God! So, there will be next time?", He lay on his bed made of boxes, and place his hands between his knees. I smile, I look back and whisper "Goodbye for now sir".

I got the job. I run to my mom. She quickly hugs me in her warn arms. Arms that makes me feel whole again, when things are not working. Arms that give a hope that all is well, even when it's not. One thing I love about her. She taught me to never give up. The words she always tells me. "My daughter, one day your dreams will come true, I see a great woman in you". These are the words that keeps me going. Because I know she sees what I cannot see. And her words are of comfort to me. I even paste them in behind the door. I see them, read them when I wake up in the morning and sleep at night. I talk about lots of things with my mom. I can say she is my best friend. She makes tea. She knows I am feeling cold. But thank God I have roof over my head, and food on the table. Though I don't have everything I am grateful. I told her about Herman.

Things are going well. I am working very hard. My mother's words will never fall down. I say, as I am paying for fruits, that I am buying for Herman. Before and after work I still go to see him. At least now he can smile at me. He smiles as he sees me coming to him. "Hey, how are you today?", Well **Vio**, I think I am catching cold. It's getting worse every night here. Calls me Vio. "what do you have today?", Here, take. I give him a plastic bag. But the words you say, Herman "It's getting worse every night". they are hurting me. Its true Vio, it's hard, but thanks for the food. I am feeling sick sometimes. "Can I take you to the doctor?", I asks him? Please you know how expensive those things are. He replies, lifting his leg, to the other one, with one hand. I can see that he is in pain. And anyway, I am not your responsibility. I want to do this, allow me. No! Vio, I will be fine. I've been living here for many years. Now I just want to rest. See you tomorrow, if you do come. He says. Of course, I will. I kiss him.

"Hey, you are here", Says my mom. Yes, I am. Oh my daughter. What is eating you today? I throw myself in that old sofa. Its Herman. He is sick. And he can't let me help him. My daughter, I suppose he means well. You have been helping him. You buy him food, and check on him regularly. I think he just doesn't want to put much weight on your shoulder. What you've been doing for him. I am proud of you my daughter. I pray he will get better. I believe so mom. Let me go to sleep. Are you not eating tonight? I cooked your favourite, pap and beef stew. Violet you never say no to food. This Herman, situation is taking a toll on you. Mom, I am feeling fine. But something tells me that Herman is in no good condition. It might get worse than I anticipate. Here is your food, if you change your mind. Thank you, mom bye. I force my feet to walk. I am completely losing it. I feel for Herman. I close the door. And for once in my life. I pray. I don't even know how, but I just did.

Today, I wake up very early than usual. I have to go see Herman. The last time I saw him. My tears almost fell down. Though in the night they did. I step from the bus. Still a cold day. Fortunately, I am no longer wearing flip flops. I can see the place where, Herman lay. But what I can't see is the sign of him. My world crumbles, as I come close to his place. I fell down on my knees on his belongings. I ask the lady, who bakes fatcuky next to where Herman lay his head. Have you seen Herman today? No man, yesterday after you left. He became very sick. I called an ambulance. They came and took him. But to which hospital I do not know. Do you know his surname? I asks, because I know it will be like climbing a mountain to find him. Yes, I do, its **Damion**. Herman Damion. It's his name. Thank you, mam. As I am standing I see a piece of his pictures. At least it's something, that will help me to find him.

Violet, you've been locking yourself in this room. Are you fine my daughter? She asks, with her caring voice. No mom, it's been week, I haven't seen Herman. And the worst part is that I don't even know where he is; alive or dead. I say that with a lot of disappointment. Only if he had allowed me to take him to the doctor. Now look. I hide my face with a pillow and cry. Don't say that Violet. You will see him again. She assures me. Just open the door for me. Please. It's ok mom, I will come to you just give me few minutes.

So, this is it. See you next week. I tell my HR manager, as I sign a leave paper. Herman means a lot to me. I have to find him. I wake up and enter each and hospital asking for him. Finally, the security assures me that, he has seen this man before walking around. He might be in the garden. He enjoys being there. The security takes me to him, here he is. His eyes filled up with tears as he sees me. He hugs me, for the first time. He let go of me. He looks me in the eyes. Again, he gives me that hug I've always longed for. I do love my mom's hug. But hence this one, is different. I've been looking for you everywhere? You gave me fright, don't ever do this again. He dries my tears, I won't never. And I deeply thank you for looking for me. I have no one, except you.

AFTER WE SIT DOWN. Today its little bit sunny. So, its warm outside. So, are you ok? I mean are you healed? Oh yes Vio. "I am completely, He says, and let his smile follows. I can see his white teeth, and those red lips. His green eyes, as he looks at me. He is so clean. And more beautiful than I've ever seen him. his haircut just makes him more handsome. He is not that dark. But I couldn't care less. I liked his heart. He is a very humble and kind man. I still wonder what happened to him. He doesn't really want to talk about it. Hey Vio? I am ready now. I came back to my senses. I was lost in day dreaming. Hey Herm, what do you mean you're ready? I mean I want to tell you something. My heart started to pound in my chest. He sighs before he can talk. His face turns bit red. His hands start shaking. He takes off the jacket. Let's take a walk, let's go to the nearby restaurant, I will tell you.

I see, **Ryan**. My ex-boyfriend. Hey, Herman, let me say hi to my old friend. He is sitting with a lady whom I don't know maybe it's his girlfriend. I say pointing where he is sitting. He sees me, pointing at him. He pretends like he is not seeing me. But he can clearly see me. I go to where he is sitting. Hi Ryan, how have you been? It's been ages, yes it has and I'm doing all well thanks. "Hey **Lisa**, this is my ex, Violet", I went to college with her. Violet, meet, **Lisa**. Nice to meet you Lisa. We shake hands. Oh, ok let me leave you guys. See you Ryan. We did have great time but I'm better off without him. when I turn to look at Herman he is already sitting down. A spot which I like in almost every restaurant is to sit in a corner, next to the window where I can see outside. And this one is amazing because I can see a tree, bending as the wind blows. I smile at Herman as I sit down. In my mind I am appreciating the spot.

After we have ordered. Herman just looks at his food, without touching nor eating. He keeps sipping water. I then stop to eat. Talk to me Herman. I say. It's a long story Vio. Make it short, because its eating you. Well I'm doing much better now. Says Herman, as he takes another sip of water. I loved her; Herman speaks. I then sigh as I relax myself so to listen to him. She was everything to me. My first love. We were just playing like kids, but things happened and she got pregnant. Her parents threw her out. I took responsibility as a man; I did all odds jobs. In order to take care of her and our first son. I was just only 16 by the time. We went from one home shelter to another. Making means ends. I watched my dream of becoming a soccer star sailing like a ship. Luckily, I got a job at the factory. I got us home. A wife and kid, we had home. I took her back to college to finish her diploma. Well I paid for everything. Our son grew, day by day. I was happy, with the little we had.

Life is unpredictable, Vio. I hold his hands. He is trying to be the man. In a society, where men are forbidden to cry, as it shows weakness. However, this is just a myth, we all human, with feelings that gets hurt every now and then, but we grow from them. Then we all kneel down and cry, and release what we feel inside. He wants to finish his sad story; this time I give him a glass of water. A factory where I was working went bankrupt. It was then closed. I was unemployed. I went home, and she said all will be well, still she loved me. I became a stay home father, raising our second son. I was proud I didn't mind. "That's sad", I say. That's all I've got. I didn't know what else to say to him. Can I have another glass of water? He says to the waiter. Coming sir. Thanks, Herman says, as the waiter pours water in a glass.

My wife started coming home late. Having late meetings. Going out on SAT, and brought back by different cars, with fancy names. As a man, I felt disrespected, only if she could do it without me seeing anything. My manhood, was taken away from me. I know I had nothing much to offer to her, but what she did. The saddest part that still boils my blood. Hmm. Was to find her on my own house. In my bed, Vio, with another man. That still pisses me off till date. She then kicked me out, that's why you met me, in that corner shop. After all the sacrifices I made for her and our sons. "I am sorry to hear that Herman. I can only imagine what you've been through, it's painful and sad". Thank you Vio, its ok. Enough about me, tell me your story. I smile at him we chat.

I and Herman we got close and starts going out often. I perform very well in my job. So, I also have a business that makes two times than my basic salary. Even Herman, he got another job. He starts to rebuild himself, and have a new home. I reminisce on all this, me and Herman. Maybe it's just in my head nothing will ever happen. But I like the way he looks at me. Herman comes back and sit next to me. Hey Vio, I've been thinking. Oh, care to share? I say as I smile, maybe it's time. I like you, and I am falling in love with you, and I want to be with you. But its ok if you don't feel the same way. You can't blame a man for trying. I just hold his hand, and kisses him. I feel the same way too. He laughs, and we hug. We walk from the restaurant. It's getting cold out there, I say looking at him. He takes off his jacket and put it on my shoulder. The trees that I only see when I'm inside, now they are here. I point to one, which looks like it has huge shadow than the others. *"Are you thinking what I'm thinking*?" I roll my eyes to him, I sure do. He looks at me with his big, green eyes. I melt inside every time he looks at me. My eyes can't keep up with looking at him. We get under the tree; we kiss as the wind blows. His red lips, as they meet mine, *gosh, I am! I am in love with this guy*. We sit in the sand, he put his hand on my shoulder, as we watch the stars in the sky.

* ANGELA *

IT'S EARLY IN THE MORNING, women rushing to clinics for children check-ups.

It's a monthly routine for kids under a certain age to go for checkup. Angela also took her baby for a checkup; however, heirs was different from all the others. Today was a different kind of a day as there was a group of young teenage mothers sharing their stories at the clinic. Angela was fortunate enough to arrive on time before all the present parents could finish sharing theirs. Angela took a backseat and hold her kid in her arms so warmly and comfortable and listen to the last lady to share before her.

Angela just sat on the bench and greeted everyone with her beautiful smile that she gave everyone. She started sharing what was in her heart; the matters of her life. The story of her life. It all started when I just graduated from high school and had to go to the university. I had good grades after matric and that allowed me to take the BSc courses and it was my favorite. I had passion for science. I've always been intrigued by the universe. Math's and science were nothing but very simple to me and I got to even correct the teachers. I was a bright student. Top of my class. And that was my privilege because I topped all the students in my school. I always came first every time.

My family background was not a big problem, we had nothing much to shine on but I was grateful for what we had. And that never discouraged me to have excellent marks in my academics. We had no electricity at home, and that meant I should study during the day, because even we could not afford to buy a candle. Maybe the candle matters less, we slept with an empty stomach sometimes. That depend on the seasons. We lived the day as it was, without the plan for tomorrow. My grandfather deserted us and married another wife, while my mother died when I was very young. It was just me and my grandma, together with my lil Brother ***Johnson***.

It was early February and I had to go to the university, my grandma saved little money for me to go to the university, it would only cover for transport to

Johannesburg, I had no idea where I was going to sleep but I hoped for the best. The day that I had to go my grandma cooked me a homemade chicken and pap, and put it in a container and took my bag with only two dresses, Jean and a shirt. My grandma and Johnson accompanied me to the bus stop. I promised them I was going to be a good girl, who will finish her studies and take care of her family, it was a priority. And I was determined that they would not die poor I was going to change my family situation.

Then time goes by and education was still the key to success and that was stuck in my head. I got to school and was previledged enough to have got a room and a bursary, one could say I had everything but a human can never be satisfied. I took advantage of everything I had I thought it was not enough for me to live with, I wanted more. The first year was all wonderful and still managed to keep good grades and that gave me the opportunity to be a tutor for a change I thought life was simple and it favored me. With time people change or everything changed, and unfortunately time changed with me. I stopped sending letters home, I could not even visit during holidays. Life in varsity took over me. I partied all night long, changing boys like clothes.

Friend's can be the best and worse and I still don't understand why I wanted more because my tuition fees and accommodation were paid for. Maybe it's the higher lifestyle I wanted and yes, I got it. But it caused me nothing but pain and misery, and when I look back there's no rectification of what I've done. My friends wore expensive clothes, ate delicious food from restaurants. Little did I know that everything comes with a price tag. I Joined my friends for luxurious lifestyle and got myself a boyfriend. He did everything and bought more of those expensive things I wanted. But because he was a student, he was not good enough I wanted someone who was working, someone who would take me to the hotel. And yes, I went in and out of the hotels and life was so fine and education became less of priority. Slept with everyone that came along as long as they meet my desires.

I still remember this day vividly as I was trying to study but I had hangover, I was sitting by the window side of my room, and I felt dizzy. I opened the window for fresh air and it was not coming through. I decided to take a bath and slept like all the other days. I thought I would get better. In the night I was not feeling any better and the next day I thought maybe I should go for a check up to the doctor. As I was still sitting on a chair the doctor came back with the results and I could see in his eyes that he was reluctant to share with me but it was fine. He sat down and looked at me and started talking about the results. He firstly counselled me before sharing the results. The doctor said to me, *"I was pregnant and also I was HIV positive"*, my heart skipped a beat and I just put my hands on my face and could not say a single word. I felt like the Earth stopped turning. Maybe the watch was not ticking too. The doctor tried to console me and told me the way forward from there. I Just stood and left the room.

The following day, I realized that I did not even qualify to write my final exam, there was nothing left for me to do at varsity and had to go home. I had no idea who the father could be because I slept with many people. I cried, but it was helpless, I brought it to myself. I was the one to be blamed. I had to go back to that hat house I left, that I thought I could fix when I was done with my academics. My grandma and lil brother believed that I was the solution to our poverty, but instead I caused more poverty by bringing another member with no father and no money to take care of.

I board into the bus and none of my friends I ever saw after I told them of my situation, as the bus approach where I should take off, I just wished I could just travel non stop. There was no one when I got home and there was no food, I knew that the situation was still the way I left. My lil brother came home from school and asked what I brought for him, like the first days when I used to come back from university. However, this time it was different I had nothing and I came back for good. What do I say to this lil kid? I knew that our poverty was here to stay. My grandma came back to collect the woods from the bush. She was happy to see me, since I've been gone for a long time and stopped caring for my family. I sat down and explained what had happened and how sorry I was. She said nothing. But Just walked away and started preparing for supper. But by the look in her eyes I knew I disappointed her. The hopes she put on me, the prayers she made for me while I was giving my body to the world. It was the end of school and my prosperous life.

As I was still sharing my story my tears were falling to my child whom I was holding and everyone in the room was sobbing. And the worst part was that my child was also **HIV positive** and I knew that the innocent child was through all the pain because of my faults. The nurse called my name as it was my turn, and I held my child closely and walked out of the door to the room where my name was called. I loved her still.

Every day, when I looked at my child. I just wish I could turn back the hands of time and make things better. Not only for her, but all those who believed in me. My grandma and brother, they were there every step. Yet I deserted them, when the world showed me what I thought was enough at the moment. They say, "***we shall all pay for our sins***". I guess I have. But it pained me to see my daughter suffering because of my sins. She was always in and out of the hospital now and then. I went to the university but I came back empty handed except for the child. For me and her life was like waiting for death. There was nothing much to live for. Dreams were washed away. I drowned them in a lake, where no one could swim.

I thought of going back to finish my degree. But with no money it was kind of impossible. I wasted a bursary. My child needed me more. Even when I was losing strength day by day. As I get weak so was, she. My grandma was getting old too. I couldn't burden her any further. My brother was just a small kid. Innocent as he was, he deserved better. When the dawn came, we buried my kid. Her life was on my hand, and I betrayed it, by making her sick from birth. My life ended when I buried her. The only thing left was to pray that my brother become a better person. And He did. At least I saw my grandma smiling and saying words to my brother unlike to me.

Change Publication, is an independent publishing

brand.

Founded by Phumudzo Mudau. It was established in 30 March

2020. Its responsibility is to take aspects of all the books

published with us. Whereas, our aim is to attract good authors

and publish books that achieve commercial success. We carry all

aspects of publication: work to editors, designers and marketing

specialists. We understand that, many authors' especially

beginners tend to struggle financially, grammatically. But

that is where we get in; helping the disadvantaged, rejected

authors by big brands and bring their books to life.

www.ingramcontent.com/pod-product-compliance
Lightning Source LLC
Chambersburg PA
CBHW061244120726
48001CB00001B/134